On Winsley Hil

CW01429389

80 369 24 3

Some other books by Alan Richardson

The Magical Kabbalah (numerous editions)
Gate of Moon
Dancers to the Gods
Priestess: the Life and Magic of Dion Fortune – new and revised
Earth God Rising: Return of the Male Mysteries
Inner Guide to Egypt (with Billie Walker-John)
The Google Tantra – autobiography
Inner Celtia (with David Annwn)
Spirits of the Stones: Visions of Sacred Britain
The Old Sod: the odd life and inner work of William G. Gray (with Marcus Claridge)
Aleister Crowley and Dion Fortune

Fiction
The Giftie – a novel about Robert Kirk

www.alric.pwp.blueyonder.co.uk

On Winsley Hill

Alan Richardson

SKYLIGHT PRESS

© Alan Richardson 2010

First published in Great Britain by Skylight Press,
210 Brooklyn Road, Cheltenham, Glos GL51 8EA

All rights reserved. Except for the quotation of short passages for the purposes of criticism and review, no part of this publication may be reproduced, stored in a retrieval system or transmitted, in any form or by any means, electronic, mechanical, photocopying, recording or otherwise, without the prior consent of the copyright holder and publisher.

Alan Richardson has asserted his right to be identified as the author of this work.

Designed and typeset by Rebsie Fairholm
Printed and bound in Great Britain

www.skylightpress.co.uk

ISBN 978-1-908011-00-8

To the memory of the late Mary Jack, and her son Angus.
Never forgotten, not once.

The places in this novel all exist; the people are entirely fictional. Any similarity to persons living or dead is purely coincidental. 'Winsley Hill' today is the designated name for a cluster of houses on the slopes of the plateau. In 1908, when this novel is set, it refers to the entire hilltop on which the village of Winsley stands.

CHAPTER ONE

The Limpley Stoke Valley, 1990

Rosie Chant was almost 100 years old, with a scattering of thin white hairs on her upper lip and chin, fingers that curled inward like dry autumn leaves, and silver film upon her eyes that seemed to entrap her memories, but reveal nothing of her soul as eyes are meant to do. Continent by day and largely so by night, she sat in a high upright chair in the corner of the room in a kind of splendid isolation from the other residents. Flanked by a polished rubber plant on one side, and an empty bird cage on the other, she sat behind them all and made them feel uncomfortable, like the thoughts we tend to shove to the back of our minds for the sake of a calm conscience.

Rosie-in-the-Home had no written records that anyone could find, or any history that she was willing to offer. She sat in her chair and stared over their heads and out toward the curves of Winsley Hill, which rose in the near distance like the plateau of a lost world, high and steep, tree-covered and always melting, somehow, as if the sun or her fondness took away its substance. Although no-one in the Home knew, or would have cared much, she had been born upon that hill. And in the chronicles of old light (far more durable than paper and ink) she had stored away within her double-helix of toil and soil, destiny and DNA, memories of a time when she had embraced a young man, golden as a god, and come to love amid the woods, within the corn, in the days before the world itself had gone to seed.

In those chronicles of old light, which are open to us all yet found by only a few, she could look back to a time when she had first met Himself, and when the bright and dark spirits of the hill would daily come rubbing against her senses like cats. She could sit in the corner of the Home and look through walls and people, and down the long shadows of the years to read the chronicles and remind herself of a night when she had given birth to her only child, screaming and panting, weeping, delivering it herself in the darkness of her single roomed cottage while strong winds pulled at the thatch and rain seeped in through the door.

The forces of decency and justice had moved her off the hill shortly after, taking away her baby and sending Rosie to an asylum, as forces of decency and justice did in those good old days. But her soul and mind would never leave. They stayed there quite independently of her body, it seemed, and lived on within that inner helix of old light, beneath the moon, on Winsley Hill …

Rosie sat in her chair in the lounge, looking back. A door slid open and a nurse came in pushing a trolley of hot drinks. Nurse Bennet had weight and marital problems, a slight oniony body odour, and you could see the hairs on her legs pressed flat by her regulation tights, like corn-circles. She was a Scale 'A' nurse and so not a real qualified nurse, but one that was allowed to deal with a lot of faecal matter and damp sheets. She was also Rosie's key-worker as they called it, though no-one had found the key to Rosie Chant in all her 100 years, and never would.

"Rose …" she said, offering her milk in a plastic beaker and scraping away the skin with an equally-plastic but colour-changing spoon. "Rose – are – you – all – right?" she mouthed, with exaggerated lip-patterns, for Rosie had been stone-deaf since neolithic times.

No response. Nurse Bennet put the mug on the trolley and squatted in front, knees apart, spare tyres settling around her hips like spring suspension. She touched Rosie's cheek, which was fissured with wrinkles – marvellous runic tales that no-one could interpret. There was something about the old lady's manner which was unusual. A tenseness perhaps. A sense of flickering like a bulb that was about to get very bright before burning out. The others in the room paid no heed. They were watching The Generation Game because it made them laugh and so feel young again, however briefly. Two other residents had died that week but no-one was particularly upset. Death came regularly to that place, like the Bingo. In both cases there was a lot of rattling and shaking, a lot of luck and missed chances and people wishing it had been their turn.

"Rose …"

Rosie glared. Her eyes were falcon claws, swooping from a great height, silver and merciless. The nurse blushed; all her guilts rose with the blood: the unpaid car tax, the stolen chicken, the Weedol on her neighbour's lawn, and that thing with her sister's hamster and the Zanussi. She was afraid of the way that the old lady could sometimes see right through her, and know things. They all were.

"He is … he is … back upon the hill!" whispered Rosie hoarsely, and they all turned to stare for she rarely spoke. Rather did she communicate looks and subtle gestures, and radiate moods of coloured light.

Nurse Bennet tried to take her hand, make eye contact, show concern and treat her with dignity and age-appropriateness as she had learned on that one-day course for which they had given her a certificate.

But Rosie dug her long nails into her wrist and drew blood.

"Rosie!" she squealed.

Rosie knew it had hurt. She remembered pain, although pain is said to have no memory. Remembered betrayal. Could never forget despair. Oh she could cope with the spirits well enough: the bright ones that made the world sing, the corn grow, and looked after your cattle if you knew how to cajole them properly; and the dark ones that stuck to you like snot and made you feel dirty, so that you wanted to scrape yourself clean with the blade of a knife. But the ghosts of despair and betrayal and pain kept her awake at night, despite the little white tablets the doctor prescribed.

She felt herself being lifted from her chair and manoeuvred to her room. The incident would be noted. Booster injections for Hepatitis 'B' would be urged, although the management would make it clear they had no legal responsibility to pay for these. Some of them looked at her with a mixture of disgust and fear, a few with admiration and fear. Rosie didn't care. They were all beneath her. Not of her time or of the hill. A great serpent was about to swallow its own tail and circuits be created. Energies and juices would flow once more.

Somehow, in some way, The Man had come back.

* * * * * * *

In the summer of 1908, she felt his shadow before she actually met him. She was nearly 18 years old and still wrapped within her youth. Rosie-in-the-cornfield, poppies in her hair, a princess bright with summer's gold. She had seen a grass snake and was keeping very still to try and catch it with a long forked branch. Rosie had no other worries then. Men, love, treachery, death and war were all places in another country far removed from Winsley Hill.

Time and its cares did not exist, not in her mind at least.

She heard voices on the breeze but ignored them. The corn rippled like the sea and turned the light into foam. The grass snake was down there, even stiller than herself, knowing that she was watching. There was a skill in catching these creatures, she had learned. You had to turn your mind off, almost cease to exist – and then strike. Last month she had caught two and stood there triumphant, one in each hand, writhing, but the boys watching walked off disturbed, not at all impressed as she had imagined they would be.

The stalks moved and bent the light. She leaned forward, flicking her dark hair back from her eyes. On the ivy-covered dry-stone wall beyond the small pond, a trinity of crows were stretching their wings into the sun and cawing. Crows were always present in Rosie's life: fluttering, squawking, dark as her moods but able to soar, also. A great shadow touched and slowly enveloped her. It seemed to trickle down the back of her neck like cold water.

Skraaa! went the crows.

Turning to look, she started to scream and then checked herself, for Rosie-in-the-shadows never had and never would give way to panic, or let the darkness terrorise. It was not a cloud as she had first thought. In fact she didn't know what it was, or how to name it. Nothing had passed over the hill but moon, sun, stars, clouds and birds. This slow and aweful shape with its glimpses of fire was beyond her comprehension. Speechless, she looked around. Others in the neighbouring fields had seen it too. They were pointing, waving, shouting as it passed over, slowly and majestically: a hot-air balloon adrift upon the breeze, bloated and beautiful.

The crows flapped off and away. You should have seen their faces. The balloon drifted past. With the sun behind her now she could see it clearly: the colour of old blood, two figures in the basket doing fast and heroic things to control a flame, and a third man leaning over with his elbows on the side, as calm as if he had been on a veranda. He was looking down at her, and through, spearing into her ribcage and ripping it open, somehow, so that her childhood fluttered out and left room for all the miseries to follow.

She could not even see him clearly but there was an impression of light, summery clothes; a broad straw hat and a notebook in his hand, held limply over the side of the basket. She was in love at once, of course, for it took as little in 1908 to plummet from the ever-becoming heaven of innocence and childhood as it does today. The flames surged, the balloon rose. It seemed to gasp – or perhaps she did. The fields were scattered with folk, as fields were in those days when people actually worked the land, and they all waved. The flames, from where Rosie stood, seemed to rise above the man's head like some corrupt and flammable halo. The people waved even more for they adored the moment, and the corn could wait for once, for just a little while. Some of them had heard of such things. Some of them had heard of a machine in Bristol called an aeroplane. They were the sophisticated ones, which is why they waved and adored like berserk children.

Rosie and the man were still. She couldn't see his eyes, his face beneath the hat's brim, but she felt his gaze holding her like strong arms.

"Bye," she said, pulling a poppy from her hair and spinning the stalk until the petals fell. At her feet, unheeded, the grass snake slithered off under a stone.

* * * * * * *

Rosie was nearly 18 when that had happened. Her birthday, on November 25th, was also St Catherine's Day which used to be a big event on the hill then, an excuse for the traditional Wiltshire pastimes of bonfires, cake-making, and public drunkenness, although no trace of such revels can be found there now. Rather like the fate of Rosie herself, if the chronicles of old light were properly read.

When that grass-snake slithered off and took her childhood with it, she was a few months short of that birthday. She had bright blue eyes that were accented by a natural crease below her lower lids that gave the angular and almost exotic features a strange air of wisdom. When she looked at you, it was not a mere teenager looking. With her slim figure (tall for that era) and long jet-black hair cascading to her shoulders, she might have won top modelling contracts today, though she had few admirers then, when men seemed to favour rounder versions with frills, thrusting bosoms, curls, and the obligatory simper. In an age wracked by TB, some people thought she looked consumptive, although she could have run marathons and scarcely broken sweat. Today, many young men would shy away from someone like Rosie believing that they wouldn't stand a chance, that she was out of their league. In 1908, young bucks on Winsley Hill were embarrassed to be seen next to her.

She was mad, they whispered.

Sometimes she taunted them with vipers, the gossip went.

It was her hands which might have made the modelling agencies baulk. Gnarled and calloused, covered with many scars, nails bit to the quick and broken anyway – they could have belonged to a small miner. These were not the hands to stroke and smooth troubled brows or bring a man to silken-touch delight: they were for lifting and handling heavy tools, for strangling small livestock and heaving large stones to repair the walls or make new ones. They were hands for gripping and taking as she gripped onto life itself, and took its decades.

When she was in a mood Rosie radiated emotions like no-one else: good and bad and the merely wistful – and it was little to do with PMT, or politics or job dissatisfaction. When she went home from the fields that evening, much as youngsters return from a good time at the cinema, it was as though she brought electrical storms into the room with her. Her mother looked up from the fire, where she had been doing some remembering of her own, as mothers do when their mothering is past. She fumbled with the tobacco in her clay pipe, reached for a spill to light it.

Maggie Chant was small and hard; widowed but not mournful. She had much venom and occasional flashes of cruel wit and skinned cats for the fur, selling these on dark nights to a man who came from Trowbridge. She could probably have done the same to men, too. Her husband, Rosie's father, could cope with the unremitting toil of the farm labourer, and later with the cancer that made a whole section of his stomach move, as if a cat itself had taken refuge there – but Maggie was too much.

"Something's happened," said the mother, meaning sex, and wiping her lips dry with the edge of her pinny.

"Mother!" scolded Rosie, strangely prim and embarrassed, although the Lord knows she had seen enough of such acts in the fields.

Maggie dragged on her pipe, gave a righteous sort of wriggle with her shoulders. "Who is it?" she persisted, though not looking at her daughter at all.

"No-one! It was nothing! Shut up! Shut *up!*"

Nothing. A shadow from on high. A portent. She wished. Rosie flounced out again, slamming the door behind. Pots shook on the wall, smoke billowed in the fireplace.

Maggie shrugged and fiddled with her pipe, poking into the bowl while staring back into the fire, into the gold-orange caves between the burning logs where she could see a plump baby with eyes like moons and a laugh that healed. Where had that baby gone? she wondered. Sometimes she felt robbed, like one of those mothers in the old stories whose babies are taken by fairies and some awkward changeling put in its place. Maggie who could skin cats, pull root crops all day long, scythe and stook with any man, and who never allowed anyone to see even a flicker of decent emotion, loved Rosie more than life itself. Even so she felt cheated by the due processes of evolution and growth. Skin like old leather, nearly toothless, hair as lank as winter grass, she would never have another man, much less another child. She was beyond such things. She was nearly 35.

"There'll be trouble," she said, spitting into the fire and watching the blood sizzle; she didn't need Rosie's clairvoyance to know that. It was a mother's prescience, and a knowledge of the ways of life on the hill where they lived.

* * * * * * *

Half-dreaming, Rosie spent the night aloft, soaring with that man who had not yet become The Man. Well, who wouldn't? When you come late to love as Rosie did, nearly 18, it comes all the more intensely. It came with the poppies. Years later – millions and millions of years later it sometimes felt – when the nation used poppies to evoke the senseless waste of Flanders, and shed tears for a lost generation, Rosie used them to evoke her first and only love and did much the same, for much the same reasons. Waste and human folly. Bitterness and loss.

She could never quite focus on his face in those dreams in which portions of sleep and waking were mixed with the narcosis of that emotion. His features would not hold: it was like peering at a reflection in a pond, rippled by a breeze. But that was all far less important than the trembling behind her rib-cage, and a sense of radiance as though the dawn sun were in there, soon to burst up and out through her brow.

It was that which her mother had seen, yes. She was jealous, yes.

But if she couldn't see the man's face clearly she knew every inch of the land below as she floated over it in her imagination, kept aloft by love as the balloon had been by fires. At the mercy of invisible currents. She knew it all better than she knew herself.

Far below, at the bottom of her dreaming and beneath her in more ways than one, Winsley itself with its eldritch manor and headless coachmen, and somewhat gargoyled church, squatted grey and brooding in the centre of a small plateau almost ringed by the river, canal and railway far below, like the triple-strand necklace of a burgeoning new Age. Rosie soaring above, had little to do with what went on in its encircling valley.

To the south of where she hovered, half an hour's brisk stroll along the beaten track, the small town of Bradford perched on its slope, trickling down it to the distant edge of Salisbury Plain, filled with redundant weavers and their empty looms, only bursting to a kind of half-life on Thursdays for the market, and less than that on Sundays for the prayers. Conkwell, a mile west and north of her soar was squeezed into a crack in the hillside like some small burrowing creature. Murhill, on the other side of the plateau and just as tiny, caught the afternoon sun and the quarry's fine dust as earnest men hacked out what was left of the Bath stone that was in such demand then. And next to that, Turleigh, neither up nor down the hillside, neither-here-nor-there, as they said then, with its own healing spring whose properties had long since been forgotten, and troughs that served horses, young children, and the poor. And there were the other scatterings that dignified themselves with collective names such as Ashley and Haugh, as though their embryos might one day grow into something valid, although they never did, and now never will. All these linked together by a spider's web of narrow one-track roads known simply as The Lanes. All these linked together with the web in Rosie's soul, and her one-track experience.

Winsley was thronged then: three pubs, a blacksmith's, a thriving bakery, post-office, dairy, nursery, school and three churches plus a sanatorium – all crammed into an area as taut as a raindrop on a glass. But even now when the streets are empty and all of these have gone, you can stand on the slopes and see the early morning mist filling the valley like a silently churning river, and see it much as Rosie did, and realise that nothing changes much under the moon, in the chronicles of old light, on Winsley Hill.

In her day the stone circle in No Man's Land, a haunted place where three roads meet, was largely intact; the remains of a processional avenue across the fields to Conkwell were still apparent; the cromlechs near the old tea rooms had not yet been scattered into a random mess of apparently natural slabs; her grandmother could remember the well-dressing ceremonies of her youth, as well as other rites that she would hint at; while the ghosts of druids and lost deities could still be glimpsed, even by the least psychic, from the corner of the eye.

Rosie, dreaming, soaring aloft, grew from this land like the corn, and awaited her own harvest. She was a bride to it as nuns are Brides of Christ, and the marks and scars of labour on her hands and feet were stigmata of another kind.

She and her mother lived in a tiny tied cottage beyond No Man's Land, next to a pond once known as Rosie's Pond, which has long since been drained in a way that she herself would never be, before a wood now known as Rose's Wood. In 1908, when the land was as virginal and untouched as Rosie, there was nothing outstandingly beautiful about this area, although it has gained this title since, in block capitals, to stop developers. In 1908, when you worked the land as the Chants did, and got as little in return, the land was clearly a bitch. Yet they loved it anyway as only children can, no matter how cruel and senseless their parents might be.

But that night as she lay in her bed in the cramped cottage beyond the pond, trapped amid the web of lanes and paths, her mind floated high above it all and flames roared her aloft, and there was a song in her heart like a choir in passion. Again and again she looked at the dream man with his blurred dream features. *Come to me* she willed with all the witchery in her, and for which the Chants were renowned. And in 1908 it was the *real* witchery of the land and the hill, and the dragon beneath and within that she used – not the present sort with its bare-arsed games amid the maize, with head-bands and crystals and a ready supply of tissues. *Oh please* she added with an almost petulant stamp of her foot, for she hadn't lost her girlhood entirely.

Suddenly he looked up and the dream gave way to a different reality. For one second the features cleared and a face looked at her like that of a fallen angel, beautiful and cruel, unbearably proud, eyes like the sky at dawn: pale and glittering with promises. He reached and touched her cheek, his hands were ice, as though he had fallen from some great height. She woke at once of course, still feeling those fingers on her cheek, and found herself sitting up in bed, heart pounding.

Her mother, across the room and by the hearth with its still-glowing embers, was spitting into a rag and watching her. She raised one eyebrow and gave her daughter one of those disapproving sighs through the nose that mothers give.

I'll meet him soon thought Rosie, avoiding the other's gaze and hugging herself back down.

* * * * * * *

She walked the Lanes under a blazing sun, her sleeves rolled to her elbows, top buttons undone, heavy skirt soaking up the sun, the grey, dry-stone walls and hedgerows making channels as narrow as her life. She had been in the fields with the others, working on the harvest, but she dropped it all on an impulse and went off toward Conkwell. The others, including her mother, looked but said nothing. Didn't do to offend the Chants, not them. Not the mother especially, who was sucking on her lips and biting back her comment.

Rosie didn't walk down the lane to Conkwell, she strode. Bare-headed and determined, utterly blank of any conscious purpose or direction that she could have expressed, but in the grip of love and its destiny, as the hill beneath her feet knew. It had felt that life-changing gait too often and from too many others before. It also knew the slow echo of the desolate return.

The dusty, rutted road took her through No Man's Land where it bisected the stone circle and also forked off to the right, down a dark and green tunnel of trees toward Warleigh Manor, in the valley. She paused there, hand resting and tingling on a stone, and gave way to the horse and fly which was making its way up from that tunnel. The driver touched his hat-brim, the two Macleod sisters he carried gave her the slightest of nods and waves – hesitant flicks across the class barrier – their summer bonnets bright and wobbling with the suspension as the horse found its footing and accelerated out of the bend. Rosie strode along the cart tracks, stuck to the web and her fate, all her soarings useless now.

* * * * * * *

Conkwell stands at a kind of cross-roads, with all but one of the routes leading back to Winsley anyway, the fourth falling away toward the valley at an angle of what they now call 30%, which in human terms means that mothers with young babies in prams are not best advised to live at the bottom of its single street, where the ancient spring and holy well lie concealed. Rosie saw spirits at that place, which her grandmother told her was called, almost secretly, the Spring of the Green Man. She saw the spirits of those who had drunk from it in aeons past, and who still came. She drank from it often herself, as we today never would, fearing it might poison us as firmly as they hoped it might heal. Rosie stood at the crossroads and looked down towards it but there was no-one to be seen there or in the houses which lined either side.

The fly was turning awkwardly to make its way back, the horse almost stepped on her foot, the driver tipped his hat again in silent apology. And somewhere behind her, like brush-strokes on the warm canvas of morning, she could hear the crows. For the first time since his shadow had touched her, Rosie was uncertain. Time, which had never been particularly mobile on that hill anyway, stopped completely for her now. She wiped her brow with the large head scarf she had loosely knotted around her neck, smoothed back her hair from her brow as fiercely as any nun might, and cursed herself for not having washed it this morning.

Where? she thought, almost desperately, but again she moved on impulse on and down into Conkwell itself, heading for the well.

*   *   *   *   *   *   *

The house beyond the well was called The Old Tea Rooms, and owned by people so confident of permanence that this name was chiselled into the lintel shortly after it opened, the prices engraved on labels of brass inside the door. Rosie had cleaned in there once, as a child, and earned a penny for a full week's work. Since then she had never done more than peer through the glass as she walked past.

There was a noise from the house like bees – the muted chatter of the shy English. All of Conkwell must have been there, or in the garden behind. Two dozen members of the great and good.

Rosie couldn't keep herself from that honeyed gathering. Despite the sun reflecting on the glass and turning many of the window-panes into sheets of pure silver, she glimpsed a man inside with his back toward her, yet wearing that summery jacket, and holding up what seemed like some antlers to general and infinitely polite merriment. Her heart rose and then stopped, like a ship acrest a great wave. She swallowed, stepped forward to peek more closely and —

"God!" she cried. "Oh hell oh hell, oh shite and buggery! God, god, ah god!"

The nail had sunk an inch into her bare left foot, she danced in pain, making her way to the well in awkward hops, a trail of blood in the grass. She put her foot into the little trough next to it and pulled out the nail, turning the water red, though not as red as her face when she heard the sniggering behind.

"You should let me do that," said a man's voice, only she didn't understand it, had never heard an accent like that before. Without turning Rosie knew it was her man. The Man. He said it again, more slowly, as if he had encountered this problem before and knew that the natives needed time to adjust to his speech as we would tune in a radio today. On Winsley Hill, in 1908, no-one had ever heard an American accent before. Behind him, and source of the sniggering, the two Macleod girls at the front of the crowd which had ambled out in curiosity.

"Allow me, miss," he said, taking out a handkerchief of pure silk and binding it deftly around her foot while she hopped and balanced on the other, too shy, too discomfited to rest a hand on his shoulder as he kneeled before her.

His hair was the corn, he reeked of smoke as almost all men did in those days. His hands were as icy as in her dream, and when he stood up and their eyes met, her legs quivered for reasons that were nothing to do with having stood on a nail, and for a brief moment the world beyond did not exist. Rosie and The Man, in the little hollowed space before the stone-enshrined spring which trickled from the side of the hill and gave Conkwell its meaning. It was the best few seconds of her life.

The elder of the two sisters sniggered again, breaking the spell, whispering something to the other. They were the daughters of Black John Macleod, self-styled on account of his moods, whose whole family was regarded as somewhat cracked even by the standards of the English upper classes. Even so, Rosie plummeted, a worm which had been dropped from a crows beak and a great distance. She wanted to slither into the ground as she saw herself the way she fancied they saw her: barefoot and rough-handed, clothes as old as the century. Them in their height of fashion, new as the day, all bows and curls and colours. But in truth Rosie could have passed today for one of the designer-scruffs that litter the glossy magazines, her simple clothes made chic by the presence within. The twittering sisters, with all their (as they imagined) Parisian style, would be impossibly dated by the time of the Great War: Rosie in her rags was eternal.

She might have blushed: her mother often said she did – an accusation which angered Rosie more than others. She didn't believe it anyway, and never had a mirror to check. Rosie flashed the sisters a look of pure venom, the fangs of her eyes biting into them both for the briefest of moments so that they winced, visibly. She lost the moment completely then. When she turned back to look at her man he was already moving away and ushering the group back indoors.

"Goodbye," he said, without a backward look.

Rosie in love came a whisper. It might have been from the sisters, through an open window; it could have been from the hill itself.

And so she was, and would be, for the next thousand years.

CHAPTER TWO

Being in love lasted 82 years. From the day it happened, when the corn was gold and she was touched by shadows, the century started to slither, crawl, take its first few hesitant steps – and then grow wings to fly. Rosie-in-love, who would one day shake hands with women who had walked in space, thought nothing of all this. She was indifferent to the progress, the change, the disasters and despair, and all the billions of acts of individual and mass cruelty which gave the century its tone. Rosie-in-love was lost within the hill; she had taken the dragon's dark place underneath the chalk and set the beast free.

It's all my fault she often thought, when the television news flashed up images of disaster and desolation into the lounge of the Home. *Where would they all be without me?*

When she first came to the Home, referred and funded by her local authority, she was a mere 90 years old and very ill. No-one gave her more than a few weeks to live. The Home, a fairly exclusive one with quality brochures, many individual bedrooms and a visiting hairdresser, had acted on compassion, making sure that everyone knew about it. But Rosie sat in the corner and recovered, miraculous but immovable. She looked through walls and sucked at the vision of the hill itself, and renewed herself daily.

Most of the other residents were retired gentlefolk of a certain kind, their double-barrelled names pinned like flags to the rooms, rosters and underwear. Rosie fell foul of these but not because of her social class: after all, longevity with its failing eyes and ears that no longer register accent, social nuances or cheap cotton, and the bladder problems and falls which obviate breeding and bank balances, will always be the great leveller.

No, she fell foul of them because of her power.

It was Ms Flyte, a much-certificated and well-connected Junior Manager who felt the lash first. There was some low-grade pushing and shoving involving a chocolate pudding in a shiny metal bowl on a slippery table-top. Rosie, being deaf, was hard to cajole and it really wasn't in Ms Flyte's job description to be doing this anyway. The pudding ended up on the floor. Rosie glared, and no-one had ever seen so much change in a face before, or such venom; it was like watching stone come to life. She straightened her already impressively straight back and gave a curious gesture: two fingers on her right hand making a slipping gesture on the palm of her left.

"That's sign language!" cried Eleanor Brittle, a newly-appointed nurse who had been on a course for communication with the deaf and disabled. "The two fingers are legs, the palm of the other hand a surface. She's talking about slipping or falling!" Eleanor Brittle was excited. She felt that she had made a breakthrough. Moments later the combative Ms Flyte, a young woman who felt that she had a brilliant future in geriatria, slipped and fell down the stairs, breaking one arm and dislocating a shoulder while ripping the padding from her new Laura Ashley jacket entirely.

Whiskered heads of both sexes turned and shared glances: longevity often brings with it a sense of omens.

On a later occasion, after a time of heavy winds and following a similar fracas with someone else's visitor, Rosie made a sort of tree shape with her right hand and forearm and brought it crashing down on her left hand – and a small tree did exactly that to the man's car as he cruised at a regulation 5 mph down the drive.

The same eyes met and eyebrows raised. Crows could be heard from somewhere. Suspicions were more or less confirmed and the Home had something worthwhile to gossip about at last. But did she see or did she cause?

Eleanor Brittle, who had recognised the hand gestures as sign language and spoke of iconicity and classifiers so that the other staff nodded and were terribly impressed, and all felt that they had a right little chancer in their midst, grew frustrated at Rosie's refusal to sign back or explain, or initiate communication.

It happened again and again, but there were other powers too. At times when she napped in her chair in the corner of the lounge a soft light seemed to play around her whole body (though not everyone could see it) and the very air had a lilt which made minor aches and pains flit away (though not everyone heard the song). And at odd private times when a member of staff had come to work straight from some domestic love-crossed disaster, Rosie would sense it and come up to them with the gentlest touch, a curious tactile blessing given with the most compassionate of faces, before going off to her room without a backward glance. Rosie knew things, saw things. Rosie was a presence within the Home, at the foot of the hill.

Some grew cautious in their dealings with her. Left her well alone. Others, who saw malice instead of power, coincidence instead of control, felt that she sneered down at them from great heights. But they were wrong.

Rosie dwelled in darkness and old light within her hilltop visions. She peered out at them from hidden caves.

*   *   *   *   *   *   *

Not counting the dreams, the third time she saw the man had been like that: his face contorted as he crawled out of Jug's Grave – a prehistoric mound that was almost lost within the woods near Rosie's home. It wasn't prescience which had drawn her there but her mother's laconic comment: "He's in the woods," as she came in from the milking and spat into the fire in a way that her daughter thought disgusting. Rosie who was in love and who had come to concern herself about manners, put on her best and only shoes and went.

*   *   *   *   *   *   *

The woods stretched along the edge of the plateau from Conkwell to Farleigh Wick. Only children went in them in daytime; only poachers at night. Some areas were felt to be haunted. Grandparents and great grandparents talked of witchcraft, but all Rosie ever saw were the People. These were real enough to Rosie: tall, elegant beings in pure simple clothes of pastel light, whose voices spoke to her from far away, thousands of years away, so she could never quite tell you what they said, though she understood the tone.

They were there now, grouped around the flesh-and-blood men excavating the grave. They were agitating like flames. And despite his contorted features as he wriggled and slithered from the hole they had cut, Rosie-in-vision knew that he too could see them. Their anger made the skin prickle like frost. Some of the men were pulling their coats about themselves, although it was a warm summer's day. Her nipples went hard; she could have killed them, but crossed her arms instead, which gave her an angry, confrontational air.

A few faces turned her way but back again, indifferent. This was the work of men, the passion of gentry. Nowadays they would use small trowels and soft brushes, and take immense pains when opening such a thing, rather like the way courtships went in 1908. But in Rosie's day they used picks and shovels to uncover the earth mysteries, setting about it all like the courtship methods of the 1990s, and then standing about smoking heavily, talking brave, and wondering why they couldn't stop shivering.

She came closer to look. The men ignored her. What did a woman know about death and inhumation, the past and its glories, eh?

"What do you know about this?" asked the man, and repeated himself as before so she could adjust to his accent. Rosie took a sharp breath. She hadn't believed, at first, he was actually speaking to her and indicating the grave with its hollowed side.

"Local traditions are often priceless sources of information," he explained to the men, as they drew on their pipes and cigarettes and nodded.

What did she know? thought Rosie, trying not to put weight on her sore foot. She knew that on certain nights of the year when the mood and sight was upon her, the woods at the place disappeared and there was open hilltop, and she saw the round houses and the folk who lived in them, the moonlight on the thatch, the shadows and the trackways, the cattle and the brindled pigs, the babies crying in the night, the palisades with the spiked heads atop, and the laughter of short lives rising to the moon …

"Nothing," she lied. She couldn't tell him, not with the men around, about the Lord and Lady who lived in the mound, whose minds had touched hers like feathers, with white-gold hair and eyes like the cold March sky.

He shifted his weight and mirrored her own posture exactly. When he moved slightly so did she. Rosie felt that he knew exactly what she was like, and what she wanted. His gaze was like a caress, he seemed to stroke her into confidence, the embarrassment at Conkwell had happened in another world.

"There are the bones of a man and woman in there," he said, indicating the grave. "They are thousands of years old. Do you know of any local myths, any stories, any lore?" His voice was gentle but she understood the challenge beneath. He was of her kind, after all.

"I … I know that if you sit in the hollow side, under a full moon in May, you can get dreams of your future husband."

No sniggers this time: belly-laughs from the men of substance, one of them making an obscene wiggling gesture with his middle finger when he thought she wasn't looking.

The American's eyebrows raised; he turned on the group.

"And I thought the men of Wiltshire were gentlemen," he said, softly enough, but there was steel in his words. In 1908, all men wanted to be

22

thought of as gentlemen, and him being an American made them all feel a little closer to that state.

You should have seen their faces! thought Rosie then, and tens of thousands of times in the decades to follow. He became at once The Man in her life. No-one had ever stuck up for her before except her mother – and that counted as little to teenagers in 1908 as it would do today.

"I will not embarrass you by asking further," he said, coming a step closer, almost conspiratorial. She smelt the wonderful stink of cigarette on his breath. Their eyes meeting, she blushed; it was a like a high tide on the sea she had never seen but somehow understood.

He brushed the earth from his shirt and trousers. Someone handed him his hat and jacket. Another sidled up in a kind of indirect apology and said: "Eh, show 'er this then, Mr Grahl," and Rosie's heart leapt, for getting a name was like finding a jewel. 'This' was a small, round and silver talisman, the size of a half-crown but probably worth a small fortune by our standards today. It had the pattern of an equi-armed cross tapped or engraved in the thin metal, and various zig-zags around the rim. Rosie reached for it but stopped. She could hear the crows. Wind rose in the trees and the sun went in. She drew back her hand sharply.

"That should never have been taken," she said to the portly man who proffered it, using the scorn for which she was well known, but which she would never show to The Man himself. "It's the Luck … the Luck of the hill. It should stay forever." She scarcely knew what she said; perhaps she merely echoed other voices.

The Man nodded once, like a hawk stooping. There was a gleam in his eyes as if she had passed a test. Rain started, slanting down, the leaves of the wood muttering loudly under their impact. The men clutched their hats and buttoned up their coats.

"Always happens," said the one with the pick, who had opened such graves before.

Rosie, rooted, watched them gather up and go. The Man turned to her when the rest had gone on a short way. He didn't need to hold onto his straw hat at all, there was an air of calm around him.

"I will be meeting you again Rosie Chant," he said, and his knowledge of her name was like an enchantment, there was no turning back after that. She would be under his spell for the next 82 years.

* * * * * * *

Rosie glistened. Such movements as she made came from a sinuous, sensuous, rippling of her memories. She became one of those great serpents which swallow their own tails: past and future conjoined; male into female forever; the old wise girl embracing the young foolish hag.

If, as she walked the Winsley Lanes in 1908, Rosie sensed a Presence more persistent than the others, then it might have been herself: the ancient girl and utter stranger who had left the hill but still remained, watching and merciless in the purity of her remembrance.

As she left Jug's Grave and trudged home along the edge of the wood, leaning hard into the teeth of the squall and even harder into the afterglow of The Man's words, she paused for shelter under the canopy of an old, weary oak. Here, unseen as she thought, she glistened and she glowed, dancing lightly between the huge exposed roots, a little jig of delight, the last show of the child she had been. The malign storm, the taking of the Luck didn't worry her enough to spoil the moment. The morals of early archaeological methods were hardly her concern; likewise the outrage of spirits. The wind whipped the rain across the field in phalanxes, like Roman soldiers streaming into battle. She danced among the roots. She danced to the song of the oak and thorn and the sharp spikes of love.

"Hello love," said a soft voice behind.

Rosie started, tripped on a root and fell full force into the man's arms, looked up and then beamed when she recognised him.

"Oh … hello Charlie," she said, friend to all the world as only people in love can be. She straightened herself, brushed the sodden hair from her face. "Just, erm, just trying to get warm …"

He let go of her, though not quickly. His hand had touched her breast as she fell, he'd never known the like. Never seen a more radiant face so close to his. Told himself the shining was for him.

Rain beat down. The cornfield before them was an ocean, frothing and churning. Another gust, driving them both back under the branches, against the trunk where she stood next to him, almost touching, her hair in rat-tails, secure within her Mystery and love's design. And Charlie Kellaway with the rain dripping from the brim of dad's old bowler, teenage bristles scattered thinly on his chin and lip, took it all for himself, like a thief.

When he looked at her, taking sly glances, he suddenly looked at jewels.

"Fag?" he offered, seizing the moment as best he knew, embarrassed and trembling at the back of his knees. Rosie, who had seen The Man smoking, who had smelt the reek on his clothes and breath and in his hair, would love one.

"You're shaking," she said softly, tenderly, thinking of Mr Grahl so not entirely there, holding Charlie's dirty, battered, cut, old-man's hand and taking one out of the packet for himself.

"Cold," he said, and he couldn't believe his luck, for no-one had spoken to him like that before. He'd never drawn warmth from any woman except his mother – and she didn't count.

Charlie Kellaway was no mystery to Rosie, though. A year older, they had been at the same school. He lived in a cottage only slightly grander than hers, but with three brothers. The Kellaways and Chants worked the same fields for the same employer for the same pay, but no love was ever lost between the elders of the tribe. Charlie with his old hat, older fustian trousers, his handed-down and over-large tweed jacket and tackety boots, and long nose which fell from a sloping brow in an almost continuous line, was of the hill. She hardly knew he existed.

Rosie held the cigarette awkwardly between her lips, tilting it up and down in search of naturalness and elegance. He struggled with his matches, they had to huddle head-to-head, shoulder-to-shoulder, to keep the light.

"Suck," he said kindly, for she merely kept the tip there, lung-pure and ignorant. She sucked and sucked again, the fag-flame bringing her ever nearer to The Man, as she thought. Charlie blinked hard. He had long lashes and pale blue eyes and lips like a girl, and no girl had ever looked at him twice. He never wanted this to end.

They stood silently and watched, the storm easing slowly as each burned inside quite as brightly as the cigarette, wrapped in their dreams as their space was wrapped in smoke.

"Thanks Charlie," she said, putting hers down and stamping on it the same way he did. Giddy, she stepped on and over a slippery root as she went past him, unbalanced a fraction and touched his shoulder again to right herself, giggling. To Charlie, who had never known a woman's touch and now had known it several times, it was like a benediction. He nodded dumbly, though at what he couldn't have told.

"See you," she said, before squelching off across the field without a backward glance.

And he was lost from that moment on, too.

* * * * * * *

In the Home, Rosie started doing sums. She did them on the edges of newspaper to the ire of the owners, on misted-up windows, on scraps of paper of any kind, and indeed on any surface which would take the felt-tip pen she had stolen from the Manager. The staff called it her 'numerical obsession' because that was a sonorous phrase which had a substance and ring to it. They felt it was something to do with her age, or her left-brain activity, or a mental compulsion akin to a tic. But to Rosie it was a means of evoking other worlds and lost souls, as she strung the sums together like those medieval talismans which sought to control spirits using Magic Squares.

When she had the clear witch-knowledge that The Man had against all expectations returned to Winsley Hill, her calculations exploded like fireworks. In 1990 Rosie had no contemporaries in the land. Anyone who had lived on the Hill at the same time as her would have been mere infants when she knew them. All others were dead. She had never witnessed their passing, never been told, but the laws of age and mathematics made it all a certainty. Her sums snaked around the possibilities: that The Man, aged 110, had somehow survived; that her calculations and her own age were wrong – after all, she didn't *feel* 100 – but here she stopped, for she slithered up against the rocky notion of her son, taken so cruelly, yet to her immense relief at the time. Rosie couldn't, wouldn't, calculate him into existence again. She couldn't, wouldn't begin to study how old he would be if he were still alive. Always because of this, her sums stopped in mid-flow.

"What's it all mean Rosemary?" asked Miss Brittle, fresh from her starter course in geriatrics, kneeling next to her chair, angling the sheet of paper toward her with a fingertip. She had auburn frizzy hair, gaunt cheeks, and a vegetarian dog which ate the Home's cat-food whenever it could. "Means what?" she added, signing it and voicing it according to the grammar and syntax of British Sign Language.

Rosie took her pen and jabbed it sharply onto the back of the younger woman's hand, leaving a scar like an exclamation mark when she pulled away with a gasp.

"At least I got a reaction," said Eleanor at a later staff meeting, positive to the last. The rest nodded, agreed, yes that was good, they said, not wanting her to claim the moral high ground entirely for herself.

And Rosie carried on with her numbers, looking for that equation which would heal the years and her own emptiness. She knew that there was not much time left in which to act.

* * * * * * *

Strange days, strange nights, on the top of the hill, in the heart of Rosie's mind. A comet was seen near the moon on three successive nights; a meteorite shower smashed into the pond and sent plumes of water dozens of feet into the air; a flock of weird birds with flame-coloured breasts landed in a field near Hartley Farm and preened themselves for a morning before flying off eastward; balls of coloured light were seen (by respectable and sober observers) to float among the trees at Inwood, where Jug's Grave had been opened; the Reverend Walter Hamilton-Smith was heard to talk in tongues ... And all the while Rosie and Charlie's faces were alight with love – though facing different directions.

Sunday was the big day on Winsley Hill. The lanes were filled with people ambling in toward St Nicholas' church, which had been built in the Perpendicular style when that had been all the rage, with a detached tower that Rosie's grandfather had helped join onto the main body of the building.

Rosie walked there alone: her mother had become lazy, and was staying in bed with her gin. She wore her headscarf and Sunday best. Her boots had been well-polished, her skirts and blouse neatly pressed by lying them folded under the carpet for a whole day. She could hear the systole and diastole of her own heart as she walked toward the sound of the three pealing bells, but the last soul it beat for was Jesus. Rosie Chant, who went to church on occasional Sundays in 1908, had the vision of Two Worlds but no religion; the muted converse with spirits, but no sense of deity. Jesus just bored her. Jesus was an empty room of dust, the smell of old wood, and the singing of hymns that no-one could possibly whistle, followed by sermons which shot over her head – but which at least led onto the gossip afterward, in the churchyard, amongst the listening dead.

The morning glistened. The hedgerows sang with birds. She felt as light as the sky and bright as the day, as if she had been transformed into pure spirit herself, and breezes flowed through her with the sun.

Living on the hill did that to her at times. As if the earth beneath had only loaned her some crude matter for the sake of a life, and borrowed it back from time to time. In the decades which followed, as her body paced up and down the long, artificially-lit corridors of Devizes asylum, the narrow walls echoing with the sounds of schizophrenia, dissociation, and breakdowns generally, her true soul was here, between the high hedgerows, winding her way to love and its chances.

"Oh, er, hello Rosie," came a voice behind.

She paused, turned to look and nod at Charlie and carried on walking, not really wanting to be seen with him but not wanting to spoil the day by being cruel to him, either. That his being there was no accident, that he had been waiting for almost two hours for this chance encounter, would have surprised her immensely, though touched her not at all.

"I'm going to church," he said, with what he hoped was the zeal of God and the sound of old habit in his voice. He had misread her dreadfully.

Rosie nodded, increased her pace. She didn't want to be with him in case The Man saw, and drew wrong inferences. But Charlie kept up. They were of the same height, though she had longer legs, and so the grace was all hers, the awkwardness entirely his. He had to pull the hat down firmly onto his head to stop it wobbling off.

"Fag?" he offered, on the move. She thought of Grahl again, and she was so transparent by now that Charlie could feel the sudden change, the surge. "Hell, you can have the lot, the whole packet. I got plenty, honest. No really I have!"

She took it, thinking of Grahl, and because of that she went all bashful like after a first kiss, and she could have done anything with Charlie then if she had known, or wanted.

"Thanks," she said softly, putting the tube of five Wild Woodbines away into her pocket, unopened, and Charlie saw what no young lad upon the hill had ever seen: the shy, wild being who on occasions had more spirit than flesh.

A breeze rippled the wheat in the fields at either side, the poppies surged like his own blood. He could never see that sight again without evoking something of that moment. Nearly a decade later in Flanders, with shrapnel embedded in his calves and the stink of death everywhere, and more corpses around him than Rosie had ever seen in her long, long life, the poppies would speak to him too, as they did to Rosie.

* * * * * * *

As they approached the church they separated. For his part there was propriety to be considered, and family rifts, and the pressure of peer groups which thought she was a bit of a dog, as they would say now; but not least because she moved away exceedingly fast when he was looking elsewhere.

The church itself was filled, as they always were in 1908 before the advent of garden centres and shopping malls. They each found a place to stand, far apart, at the rear. Holding 250 at a sitting it was as filled with the hierarchies of the hill as some imagined Heaven to be with angelic orders. No seraphim or cherubim in those choice pews at the front but the Brinkmans, Poores and Knatchbulls, whose presences would awe Rosie as no bright or dark spirit ever had. And there at the front, classless in his own way, was The Man, head tilted politely to one side as Lady Vesey-Jones whispered in his ear.

Thank you said Rose with a blink of both eyes and a nod of her head to the un-named, unseen and unimagined Power which probably stalked the Winsley Lanes, oversaw all things upon the hill, and which had brought her to this pass. She didn't think of it as a God to be worshipped but more as a useful energy which should be respected. If they had had electricity upon the hill, and in her cottage, she would have said as much to the light switch, and for the same reasons.

The service. The prayers. The song and the wheezing of the organ exactly as church organs were meant to do in small villages, in 1908. The arrows of the sermon, barbed with Latin and some Greek, whistling overhead … And then the Reverend Walter Hamilton-Smith high in the pulpit, introducing them all to their learned guest, a Mr Edward Grahl from America, and the way he said that last you just knew that he saw it as a small and decayed suburb in Purgatory.

Grahl nodded but didn't stand, or turn. In fact, as Rosie and a few others noted it was the only time he lowered his head during the whole service. And nor did he take the Communion wafer itself, but remained in his place while the others shuffled and edged past him, apologising as only the English can.

No need for that muttered some of the congregation.

After, among the flaking tombs and beneath the ancient, poisonous yews, the people moved back and forth within the precincts in that queer and vigorous Brownian motion of gossip, catching up on the real things which mattered on that plateau.

"The reverend, 'e doan't like 'im," she overheard. "Come to look for his Norman ancestors!" said the man in surprise, as if the obvious place to look was in Bradford market every Thursday morning where they and everyone else would surely be strolling around.

"He's actually a scholar," said another with a don't-ye-know? air, fiddling with his watch-chain. "He's researching folklore and prehistoric remains. He's writing a book. He's toured all over Europe interviewing peasants."

Well, she couldn't help him there.

"Good to see you Rosemary," said the vicar, although it was a sour kind of welcome that his voice offered. He had heard about Rosie. In fact he had enough feyness himself to recognise it in others, though he greatly feared those realms into which the young woman was said to peer.

Rosie briefly bowed her head. She never knew how to relate to the classes above her, and simply looked away and around the throng with that bland face that others took as haughtiness.

"Is your mother any better?" he asked, though his mind was still worrying over his sermon as no-one else's was.

She frowned but shrugged, nodded anyway, thinking he was making some socially snide observation. Better than what? she wondered, better than who? She might have said something then but The Man came past, crunching on the gravel path, the Macleod sisters flittering at either side like sparrows after the frost, giggling as ever. Black John himself followed on after, panting like an old bull, red-faced, jabbing his stick into the ground at every step.

"Hello Rosie," came the voice from behind, in the tones of the Hill, under the shadow of the yews. Even though she knew it was Charlie she turned momentarily and lost that fleeting chance to make eye-contact with Grahl, who strode on past with his retinue without acknowledging her at all.

"Good sermon, eh?" the boy said, his shoulders back, ignoring the sneers of his contemporaries beyond the wall, the scorn of several aunts and one uncle, but going all out for love at all costs, and magnificent enough in his own simple way if only she could have seen it.

"Would … would you, er, come to the dance with me at the Hydro?" he asked, his circulation doing strange things below the skin of his face, his throat dry and heart pounding.

Rosie didn't look at him, she daren't. Didn't want anyone else to see her fury. So she found interest in scuffing at the long grass which curled around the edges of a tomb, safe from the scythe. Anyone who didn't know would think she was blushing.

She's blushing, thought Charlie, every part of him quivering.

She looked up quickly and then down again, as people around were pretending not to notice but were all ears.

"I'll walk with you on Hell first," she muttered, and strode off.

Charlie nodded, let her go, took a great drag on the morning as he would a first cigarette, and felt like singing. One of his aunts, who had known much love herself and had no time for family squabbles, sidled over and asked:

"What did she say? Will she go out with you?"

He went all shy, but smiled. "Yer, she wants to go walking on the hill with me."

* * * * * * *

"She's taken to wandering," said the matron. "We found her down the drive in her nightdress. If she ever gets onto that road she'll kill herself, and then who's to blame?"

"We can't lock her in," said the Manager, who understood what the other was angling for. "We are not registered for that. We are not allowed to lock any resident in."

"But we must do something. This is happening more and more, we just can't cope. We have to do something."

"She's 100," said the Manager, meaning that time was on their side.

"She's strong as an ox."

"Matron, we cannot lock her in …"

And they couldn't, and no-one could, for Rosie went where Rosie wanted, always within the geography of her consciousness that shaped as Winsley Hill.

In the previous days there had been heavy rains. Flood warnings in nearby Bradford-on-Avon. The road to Staverton was closed. The fields near Limpley Stoke, leading up to the Viaduct, were awash. The stream which flowed past the Home, normally grey and placid, was gorged and boiling white and roaring now, creeping closer to the door. Sleep was disrupted. Residents complained. But Rosie was close to being ecstatic.

Water is a symbol, Rosie, Grahl had told her once. *It is a symbol of our consciousness, and what lies below it. Do you understand?* She nodded, not understanding at all. At least not then, not in the summer of 1908. Aeons later she understood exactly. She had preserved his words so perfectly, replayed them so exquisitely, that wisdom came with repetition.

She stood in her rayon nightie, on the bank of the stream in the pouring rain, lightnings flashing over the hills near Conkwell, nipples hard and juices flowing freely, breathing heavily and eyes alight, with the water pouring down her body and off her bare legs and feet, onto the bank and into the stream. The extraordinary weather of late had nothing to do with meteorological disturbances over the Atlantic or Azores or anywhere else but here. It was all to do with Rosie herself, for Rosie and the land were one, and even the crows were silent. Water is a symbol of consciousness, and what lies below it.

Back in the Home, where she had not yet been missed, the lights flickered, the washing machines flooded the laundry floor; an overflow tank in the loft leaked and wrecked a room below; water was heard gurgling in plug-holes while the pipes and valves made strange noises generally, and more old men than ever before were wetting their beds. Plumbers were called, along with specialists in enuresis. Insurance policies were taken from locked filing cabinets and scrutinised. Sandbags were made ready and weather bulletins were checked at hourly intervals. But Rosie, who was soaked inside and out by this downpouring of consciousness and what lay below it, raised her arms to the lightnings and, with a rusty throat, made the sort of noise that pterodactyls might have made before swooping to kill, in a pre-human world, at the leathery end of time.

* * * * * * *

One Monday, at dawn, when Rosie had only just got dressed and pulled on her dead father's old army coat ready for work, and when a lone cockerel stood on a wall exulting as the sun rose somewhere behind the Dog and Fox, at the far end of the Lanes, Grahl appeared on Rosie's doorstep.

"I've come to take you walking on the hill," he said, as dark birds *skraaa-ed* in the field beyond and pecked up worms with bloody beaks.

Rosie, fluttering at her hair and sucking the bad taste from her teeth, suddenly felt that her working clothes were sticking to her like a great scab.

All had been pre-arranged with her employers, the Potticks, who would be compensated for the loss of labour: she, Rosie, would be paid 30/- for the loss of a week's work.

"You too," he told the mother, who stood in the shadows of the cottage, half-dressed and lazier than ever, as Rosie thought, pale as wax and shaking – but eyes like swords anyway. He needed her local knowledge, an hour or so each day. For his research.

They were to consider it a paid holiday which, in 1908, was a concept so alien that he had to repeat the term three times. The older lady pursed her lips, shrugged. She had seen his type before: the higher classes of men breaking themselves in on lower class women. She gave him one venomous but impotent glare.

"I know what you're after," she said, then closed the door upon them both and went back to her bed.

"Sorry, sir," Rosie said, unable to look him in the eye. "Hope I never get like that when I'm old."

And nor did she.

CHAPTER THREE

If you were to get a human heart and cut it open, and keep one half in an atmosphere which would let it dry out but not rot, then you would see a pattern within its exposed and shattered chambers like the lanes, fields and ways around Winsley. Even now, despite the surgery of the by-pass, Rosie would still recognise it all: her own cut-open heart seeking its own kind of by-pass in those last days.

When she went a-walking with Grahl that first time she had never thought about these patterns consciously, never had any sort of map of the hill within her mind that she could have drawn out. One place led into another and into another, and the links were of people and experiences, rather than roads. When it came to taking Grahl around the hill she wasn't quite sure where to begin.

"So this is where it all begins," he said, outside her cottage at dawn, all jaunty and cocky but looking keenly at her as if there were another meaning to his words, as if it was not about walks and geographies and jobs, but of futures that had already been formed, and he was at some vantage point.

"Well, I must change first," she told him.

"No need," he said softly, soft as the morning, looking her up and looking her down, and to Rosie's mind it was as if he had just described her as the most beautiful woman in the world, and she was melting on the spot. So Rosie with her wild hair, her cracked and bare feet, and old army overcoat, shrugged into her own formidable arrogance and strode beside him, head up and eyes flashing, as if she wore the finest designer clothes.

"Lead on," he said, and she did.

If, as they walked, he didn't say a great deal then Rosie didn't expect it anyway. They drew strange glances from others making their ways to work, for the Lanes in 1908 were filled with early risers as they never would be today. Some she nodded to, with that restrained snooty air she had; some – the Kellaways – she ignored completely. She felt them staring at her back as she and Grahl walked on past; she knew they were whispering. It was the best morning of her life.

"So, erm, what do you want to know?" she eventually asked, as they headed toward Haugh and Ashley. The drystone walls, great lengths of which had been built by her own grandparents, rose above head-height in places; they could see nothing of the land around, their attention all focused on the lightening clouds in the east, the bird-song, the masses of wild flowers which no-one thought much of in 1908, but which are protected species now.

He didn't answer straight away, but she learned that was a trait of his.

"I want to know about myself," came the eventual reply, which is a clichéd answer now but quite a startling idea when Rosie's world was young. Even so you could just tell (if you hadn't been in love with him) that he had given this answer before. He had family traditions, he said, of Celtic ancestors, who themselves had claims to Roman bloodlines, who at some point within their migrations had lived in Winae's Ley. He was tracking them down, preserving their lore. He had notions about the Spirit of Place. The more he rediscovered them, the more he understood himself. That sort of thing, he seemed to say, as Pottick's bull in the lonely field beyond the wall tilted its squat face in the air and bellowed.

Rosie nodded. Once, on a day trip with the Elementary School (in itself a radical experiment which had provoked local controversy) they had walked to Farleigh Castle, trudging down vale and up hill, clutching their cheese roll and apples for lunch. Once there they had been shown around by Miss Fossington-Gore who smelled of alsations, whose knitting poked disrespectfully out of her coat pocket and who, even to Rosie's nascent perceptions had little real idea about the castle. To her, the place was alive, still inhabited. To Miss Fossington-Gore it was just a collection of stones with some attached histories and frequent, irritating visitors.

I'm a sort of a guide, she thought.

"Can you see?" he asked.

She nodded again, understanding perfectly. But her attention was taken by a bunch of flowers left on the wall, a clumsy collection of roses and tulips, and some blue and yellow buds she didn't know at all, carefully wrapped in a sheet of newspaper. *Oooooh,* she thought, and to her heightened senses and even more heightened ideas she felt that this was a gift left specially for her, from that mysterious Power which walked the Lanes and had brought her to love. *Thank you,* she mouthed, taking the bunch to herself and trying to stop silly grins from appearing on her face. Though if her senses had been just a little duller, her notions set a notch lower, she might have glimpsed poor Charlie hiding on the other side, eyeing the bull uneasily, cursing himself for dropping them as he scrambled over, his own dawn mission thwarted by this stranger.

Charlie felt cold and sick inside. He hated Grahl at once. The concept or reality of America meant nothing to him beyond the pattern of some old maps that he had seen at the same school as Rosie. In 1908 he had never heard the term 'Yank', could never have understood the man being here. That he was from off the hill, and from another social strata, was quite enough for him. *I know what he's after* he thought, shivering, and only thankful to his own fate that he had glimpsed them first and saved himself from humiliation. The bull pawed and snorted, drooled. Charlie jammed down his hat and moved exceedingly fast, below the shelter of the wall.

*   *   *   *   *   *   *

The couple walked, Rosie clutching the flowers to her breast. She was almost sauntering by now.

"No, I mean what do you see?" he insisted, pointing to that spot in the centre of her brow which anyone today would understand, but which made Rosie start. She, who knew nothing of Third Eyes, or pineal glands, or ajna chakras or esoteric physiology of any kind, understood his meaning at once, found his symbology astonishing, and felt a sense of relief that here at last was a man who understood her, who would not be driven away by her strange faculties.

"You do, don't you? You see things. Here ..." and when he made contact with her brow the touch was electric.

She nodded, breaking the contact, blinking hard.

"Yes sir," she confessed, "I do."

They walked again, coming slowly toward Ashley.

Dogs were barking, almost baying, from within the farm. Men were in the fields and hard at it already, hitching up the workhorses. A dead crow was pinned, spread-eagled, on a five-bar gate.

"Rosie I want you to tell me what all this was like before – before all these walls and fields and farms. Tell me what it was like in the old, old days when my ancestors were young upon this hill, when they took off their enemies' heads and set them on poles, when the Moon was high and red and women tended its fires. The book I'm writing will be like no other guide book or history book you've ever seen, but I need your vision to help me. I can see a little way into the Otherworld, but not far, not clearly. Not many people understand this sort of thing, but you do."

Well she frowned, but who wouldn't? He spoke intensely, without blinking, keeping eye contact at all times. And as he spoke, pictures of just such things flashed through her mind's eye.

"But I know ways to make you see – further and better than you ever have," he added, and Rosie had never heard anyone speak like that before. Although if she had had more wisdom, or experience, she might have thought it rather practised, as though he had said this to many peasant girls with gifts like hers, on many hill-tops in his travels. But she nodded anyway, and agreed to the deal, for 30 shillings a week – a week! That, plus a dose of love that would keep her going for nearly a century would have tempted anyone in those days.

Grahl smiled – the same charming and guileless smile that she had glimpsed down Conkwell on that first meeting.

"Poor thing," he said, but he meant the crow, for he went and pulled its wings free from the nails, folded them against its body and threw it in the air like a conjuror setting free his doves. The crow thudded to the earth. Rosie smiled. Farmhands like her had a robust sort of humour as far as death and animals went. But to her astonishment the bird twitched and struggled, flapped to its feet upon the dry, baked soil and managed to make a low, clumsy, crashing flight across the field to safety.

"I thought it was dead," she muttered.

Come Rosie ... we've got a long way to go said someone within her head.

*   *   *   *   *   *   *

Each day at dawn, when the cock fluttered onto the wall and rasped its greeting, and the dogs went frenzied at Haugh farm, and the hill-top gossip rose from the lanes like the mist, she walked with him. She showed him the Lanes and the fields, the footpaths and bridleways, the woods and copses and all the secret hollows she had known as a child between Murhill and Monkton Farleigh, from Limpley Stoke to Bradford Leigh. At times, though, she scarcely knew if she was in this world on that hill, or half-way into the next, in a different Age. These were the moments when he would usher her between the whispering trees and a great stillness seemed to descend around them, like a bell jar, and he would hold her hand and tell her to *see*, and often she would. And the farms and lanes, walls and fields disappeared as he said they would, and there was only the bare, primal hilltop before her gaze, scattered with stone circles and processional avenues curving like serpents to the holy ground at Conkwell, and a great earth-covered cromlech where the church now stood.

Grahl listened as she described what she saw. Sometimes he took out a small notebook and scribbled down details. Sometimes he just stood there, eyes half-closed, swaying a little as if he shared her visions and indeed lived them with her.

And really, he could have had Rosie any time, any where, he wouldn't have had to ask, he only had to do it and she would have complied. When she came back from her visions, sucking in her breath through clenched teeth and starting to focus on the world of 1908 again, she felt like a bitch in heat, she wanted him to mount her, she wouldn't have cared who saw. Yet Grahl, who was in and out and through the levels and ways within Rosie's mind, soul and spirit, never touched more of her body than her hand.

At least not yet.

*   *   *   *   *   *   *

They walked on other levels too. Not merely the physical or psychic. With that classless American air and indefinable yet very strong reek of 'old money' as we would term it now, coupled with the novelty value of having a learned writer visit their remote Wiltshire stronghold, Grahl had access to levels of society that were forever beyond the Chants. Rosie, who could see other worlds and through Time, could never have made the leap from her tied cottage to the polished halls of the gentry without him.

I know what she's after thought Lady Vesey-Jones as a group of the local great and good had tea on her lawn, and tilted their hats against the noon sun and marvelled in their collective way at how Freshford, across the valley, seemed like a toy village in this light. Her husband Sir Charles, who had done great things in Afghanistan and been fêted nationally as the 'Man Who Held the Gates', was busy in his gardens, as he always was on such occasions. He could be seen at times on the lower slopes, down toward the canal, a tall and balding man with brown cord trousers, and collarless shirt with rolled-up sleeves, wielding a small sickle with an air of purpose, like some forgotten druid.

Grahl sat on the ha-ha in his strange light suit and Panama hat, completely at ease, holding court in a way that his hostess had never quite managed. Rosie, sitting in a cane chair a few feet away, was quietly proud of where she now found herself, and smoothed the lines of her new green dress with its little black buttons that she had bought. Grahl, in that same classless yet occasionally challenging air, had introduced her to them all as his 'friend and guide', and made them know that they had to accept her on those terms. Lady Vesey-Jones, never blessed with huge social skills, made her as welcome as she knew how.

After all, she had been a Rosie herself once, though no-one ever knew: and her husband had held the Gates a little too long to have been able to find out himself.

"So what will you call your book, Mr Grahl?"

He told her, and from the way he spoke Rosie just knew it was the greatest and most important volume ever written: 'The Oldest Faith in Celtic Lands', even greater than his previous: 'The Old Faith in Celtic Lands'. It meant nothing to her. She could not have got beyond the first sentence invoking the words of Diodorus Siculus. She loved them both anyway. One day, in that indeterminate dream-time in which she was always surrounded by strong sons, in a house full of windows and parquet floors, she would have both copies on a shelf and do her own dusting.

So Grahl yarned. His drawl was like the lazy drone of bees around the hive. He spoke of walking, foot-sore, throughout the Highlands and Islands of Scotland, getting lifts on carts or donkeys, dealing with suspicious locals and their dogs, or hacking through near impenetrable bramble to reach a near-forgotten well in a lonely valley. He spoke of simple people and their lives, old ladies and their memories, of ghosts and hauntings, demons and obsessions, and of how someone called the Reverend Robert Kirk became so obsessed with the Otherworld that he stepped into it bodily, in 1691, and afterward local women in living memory would go to his old manse and give birth in the hope of bringing his soul back into the world.

"I cannot imagine any woman doing that for the Reverend Walter Hamilton-Smith," said their hostess with unexpected drollery, and they all laughed and cups rattled in saucers in the usual English way. His tales were all the sort of low-risk, slow and lazy adventures with much dreaming and even more charm that would be made into a television drama today, and win awards for costume and landscape. There, on the lawn of Wildernesse Manor, the lesser gentry of the hill drank it all, leaning forward to catch every word. Even the servants, coming to and fro with more drinks, felt that something unusual was happening, and forgot to sneer at Rosie – one of their own kind – who sat there in her stupid fluffy dress as though she were muck.

But we've got all that here thought Rosie, remembering the things she had seen in the gaps between the worlds, at those moments when the Moon and her vision was high: echoes of the past; realms which interpenetrated ours but were as different as chalk and cheese.

"But we've got all that here," said Grahl, and he flicked a little sideways look at Rosie, so that all eyes swivelled toward her and the general fluttering of conversation stopped and swooped to the earth like a flock of birds.

Old Crows thought Rosie, wishing she could worm her way out of it. There was a silence. A predatory silence in which some comment was evidently expected from her. It probably only lasted a second – perhaps three – but to Rosie it seemed as if a whole lifetime of class antagonism was stored in those pointed looks, each one ready to peck down and slice her up for food.

"Do we really?" said Lady Vesey-Jones in an emollient tone, tucking a strand of hair under the pale blue semi-turban that was all the rage among women her age, that year. Lady Vesey-Jones was kinder than she knew. "Well I'm sure we shouldn't spoil Mr Grahl's book by pestering Miss Chant now. We can all read about it soon enough. Oh look! There's Charles … Let's see if we can't get him yarning to you all about Indi*ar*!"

Eyes turned back. The flock took wing again. Rosie was safe.

Lady Vesey-Jones *coo-eed* her husband in a way that we have long since forgotten, and would find rather strange today: a sort of post-Victorian, upper-class whale song that could carry encoded messages over enormous distances to others of the same species and with the same perceptions.

The man paused as he skirted the bramble bushes, looked up and made a brief acknowledgement before stooping to dip his handkerchief in the little stream which tumbled down the valley side, and wipe his brow with it. For a moment it seemed that he might ignore her, but she *coo-eed* again, waving the lacquered fan that he had brought from Tai-Pan, and there was no resisting that call.

Sir Charles, in his boots and old baggy trousers, lean and tanned and larded with sweat, with almost more silver hair in his nose and ears than on his head, made no attempt to return the eager nods that the group aimed at him. Ex-colonels and heroes could do that, even in a society which relied upon the lubricant of manners much as an automobile needs oil.

Grahl rose from his chair, as people did in 1908. Extended his hand in that warm, welcoming, American way of his so that you might think they were old friends meeting again after years, and not complete strangers. His hand hung there in mid-air, New World reaching to Old. Sir Charles wiped his on his trouser leg and started to grasp it but suddenly stopped, as if stung, and the reaction was so marked that some did indeed fancy they had seen a wasp.

At once the old sylvan druid disappeared and there stood a man who bristled, ramrod straight and challenging, and everyone saw that if anyone could hold gates at that moment against overwhelming odds, then he could, and no-one would *ever* get past.

Horses whinnied in the stables. Crows were heard. Far away across the valley someone was blowing a whistle to summon a cab. And Rosie, sitting on the lawn at noon, in mid-summer, could not stop shivering. She felt as if all her body heat was being drained from her solar plexus, so much that she folded her arms to cover this spot, and crouched forward as if in pain.

No-one else noticed. They were too busy being shocked, and delighted, by the sudden change in mood. And the modern world, had it been watching, wouldn't have understood her distress either, for the modern world with its psychobabble of jargon and buzz words, and its tendency to explain away the great forces of the innerworld as "nothing more than ..." has lost touch with Evil as a force, and the way it can make you pale and shaken and want to empty your guts when it is touched upon.

"Get out of my garden," said Sir Charles, with the sort of voice that you only hear on old British films now. The American lowered his hand in dismay, and at least one heart in that garden went out to him. "Get off my property and out of my valley," he added, for although he only owned a hundred acres or so of one slope, there were ways in which he was spiritual overlord to it all.

Grahl took a deep breath, clenched his fist, then nodded curtly and reached for his hat.

"Oh Charles ..." said the hostess weakly, making vague motions with her hand as if trying to catch the spirit of the exchange. All eyes were on the pair; no-one pretended not to notice. The sound of the whistle still floated across the valley; inside the manor some titled grandsons were rattling sticks on the stair rails, and a servant dropped some crockery. But in that garden, in the epicentre of silence, Sir Charles was being – as so many of the anti-American onlookers thought – quite splendid.

Grahl turned without a word and strode off up the drive, Rosie following on after, bewildered as to what had happened and unsure as to what action she should take. So she did what she felt destined to do: she followed on after him and said nothing, toiling behind up the steep hill and onto the main road, then across and into the sanctuary of the high hedges that lined the Lanes. He stopped and leaned against a large stone which had been part of a processional avenue in the ancient of days but had, by 1908, been adapted as a gate-post. He wouldn't look at her, just leaned back against the stone and rocked from side to side as if he were on a hinge.

"Have a cigarette?" said Rosie, on a kind of inspiration, and when he accepted she breathed a silent thank you to Charlie and that was as close as he ever got to her, although he never knew that.

Grahl dragged deeply and blew out smoke through tight lips, pushing himself back against the stone as if he would sink into it, balancing himself with spread legs and nothing like a hinge now but a tethered dragon, all unaware of the virgin next to him, and the virgin's yearning.

He was about to say something to her then. Rosie felt, with a leap of her heart, that it was about to be something immensely important, as apocalyptic and revelatory within her own small life as anything she had ever heard in church. There was that air about him again, the rising sense of command. He was just about to speak – he would have done – but for the sound of rustling and creaking that came toward from around the next bend. A sort of rushing and crashing as if a great leathery beast were indeed loose between the hedgerows, its wings causing havoc in its earthbound plight.

But what they saw and heard was a new kind of sound on Winsley Hill in 1908, and one still worthy of our attention as the 'Winsley Wheelers' came hurtling past en masse. Young men in caps and bright waistcoats, plus fours and stout shoes, pedalling furiously or else working their brakes to keep in formation. They had the sort of place in the public regard of 1908 that bikers have today: they were collarless scruffs and disrespectful with it. They lived on the edge and did bad things. Vergers were insulted, milk was taken from churns; silly hats were fastened on sheep and there had been fisticuffs in the tea gardens at Murhill between them and some local farmhands. One of them was known to carry Fabian Society leaflets and advocate Free Love – whatever that was. The local bobby had his hands full; there was talk of buying him a faster bike.

Whrrrrrrh! they shouted in unison when they saw our couple, flexing their arms in a universal gesture which needed no course on sign language to interpret. And there was something about the tone which evoked images of bull upon cow, dog on bitch, cock on hen, and every animal mating since time began.

Rosie blinked, blushed. Whatever Grahl had been about to say or suggest was forgotten as he smiled and waved them past, then stubbed his cigarette out on the stone. She copied him.

"Where now?" she said, although it was *What now?* that she meant, as she hugged her arms to her stomach, sealing up the hole which had been ripped in her gut by that incident with Sir Charles.

Grahl leaned forward and kissed her so suddenly that the brim of his hat struck her brow. She gasped. Hadn't expected it just then. But as she returned the kiss in her own innocent way she was startled by his tongue snaking between her teeth, showing a knowledge that was on a different evolutionary scale to hers, and her ability to respond.

"Oooh" she gasped, thinking that this must be some American custom.

And when his tongue withdrew and his face drew back he could see right through her, and he just knew how aroused she was, how ready to be covered by him, there in the gateway, on the trodden corn, careless and uncaring.

"Go home," he said, and she never forgot those words or the confusion she felt. Did he mean them protectively? Dismissively? Had she disappointed him in the kiss? Was he afraid of his own feelings? Over the decades these two words became like a Japanese koan: enlightenment, bliss, could be found if their cryptic meaning were cracked open. *Go home.* Grahl, who had come across an ocean to find his own true home at the beginning of time, was a fine one to tell her that.

She stood and looked blankly but all he did was turn and walk away in that curt style of his, and it was as if she didn't exist, for he never looked back, and you could see from the back of his head and shoulders and the way he strode that he had other things on his mind.

"Will I see you tomorrow?" she called weakly.

A job is a job she seemed to hear, though whether it was in her head or on the breeze she could not say.

*   *   *   *   *   *   *

It was about then that the mutilations started. Isolated horses, sheep, or – more usually – cattle, found sprawled in the fields with awful injuries: severed tendons, teats ripped out and tongues cut off. Three such beasts were found at scattered points upon the hill within the first week, and then once a week afterward, for months to come. People were appalled, sickened. Congregations increased; the pubs were bulging. After high level meetings in Trowbridge, the county town, an extra policeman was employed on a fixed contract to join the existing one. The two of them on their bikes, working 12 hour shifts, represented an unprecedented show of strength. Some blamed the Wheelers, and had just been waiting for such a moment. Pressure on the group became intense.

They took to doing good deeds and some of them settled down and got engaged, their wild oats firmly behind them, never dreaming that in a few short years a place called Flanders would beckon. Others blamed travellers, as people always do, and a gypsy was beaten up at Avoncliff and thrown from the aquaduct into the river below while his children watched, screaming. Miraculously he survived with only a lot of bruises, and left the area taking most of his children and one of his wives with him.

In the summer of 1908 lightnings seemed to flash around the plateau. People gossiped and muttered as they never had before.

The upper classes shook a bit, like high buildings in a mild earth tremor. There were fights in the *Prince of Wales*, down Turleigh, and regular disturbances in the *Seven Stars* which spilled onto the street. Some blamed the Fabians, who were vaguely felt to be a group of dangerous individuals who planned to unsettle and eventually conquer the entire world, starting on Winsley Hill. Retired colonels nodded over their port and made sage, knowing comments about the situation. Freemasons in Bradford held a special lodge meeting to see if they and their trowels and aprons might be of any use in such troubled times. Nothing was very solid that summer. It was not like of old, before Grahl arrived. Time seemed to begin, with his arrival. Even Charlie, smitten as ever but confused like never before, thought of leaving the hill and going away for a while. Somewhere far away and different, like Bath, seven miles down the road or half that if you cared to cut over Brassknocker Hill.

Rosie's job continued, though on a spasmodic basis; Grahl always turning up unannounced, arrangements already made with her employers, compensations duly paid, he and Rosie off for the day. So Rosie in her feyness touched stones, sat very still near ponds, dreamed amid trees, held ancient objects, and let the images float past her brow like clouds while Grahl took notes and sometimes – the best times – held her hand.

Sometimes she wondered where she was: amid the summer of 1908, or fluttering through the young world of the ancient dead until she was as well known to the latter as a shadow, as they were to her as visions. Rosie between the worlds, lost in the lemniscate. She thought it would never end, and it never did, not for her. But oh … she was desperate for the love and its consummation. She ached for it, at any cost.

"Cigarette?" he'd say.

"Yes please."

Something would happen soon, she knew. The pressure was awful. Something had to burst.

CHAPTER FOUR

When Rosie had been in Devizes asylum for over five years she received a parcel. Not many people did in that place. It was wrapped in brown paper and fastened with string in such a neat bow that everyone knew the matron had already opened it. And not many people anywhere had ever received a parcel from America. The stamps alone were worth coming from distant wards to look at.

"Here you are Rosie," said the senior physician, for it was felt that only someone of his experience should pass on such a thing to such a woman. He said it again, louder, and once more, and it was from this moment on, from his little office, that Rosie came to be ascribed as having a hearing loss. "It's from America ... America!" he said, pointing to the stamps and postmark, which was something illegible ending in an 'a'.

Rosie nodded. Rosie knew what it was. Her strange talents had increased, if anything, since she had been committed. The institutionalised life of the hospital with is own inexorable rhythms and seasons, its own tides and moods occupied her as the spirit world had on Winsley Hill: a separate place, to which she made acknowledgements, but with one side of her mind only. The doctor, who was aware of her history far more than she would have cared to know, found this all terribly interesting, as people of his ilk did in those days.

"Open it," he said, and he might have been offering the secret door into an enchanted mountain the way he said it.

Rosie undid the knot, the folds of brown paper, and sat there with the book on her lap, the small white writing on the green cover like the daisies in springtime, like the fields upon the hill. It was Grahl's book, of course. *The Oldest Faith in Celtic Countries*. Compared to the handwritten manuscript that she had once stacked neatly on Grahl's desk in The Swan Hotel, it was painfully small. Her life was in there somewhere. Her vision. Compressed into a small space with tiny print. She opened it carefully. Inside, on the flyleaf, was printed 'To the Fellowship of RC', and his name signed underneath, and the cipher $7° 4^\square$ after it in brackets, but nothing more than that.

"What does that mean, Rosie?" asked the doctor, speaking loudly.

Rosie knew nothing. *What had she ever known anyway?* she thought. Grahl was a being in another world now, beyond Time and the cold Atlantic. It was only her love which bound them. Like a pregnant mother, she was pumping everything down that thin umbilical and getting nothing in return but sleepless nights, sharp pains and bloated limbs.

"Read it to me," she said, her voice a little hoarse through lack of use.

And after checking his fob watch and looking at the pouring rain the good doctor (who was only too glad he had an excuse to be in an asylum in Devizes instead of Passchendaele) scanned through the pages and did.

"It says ... oh, let me see. Here. It says 'There was once a young woman who fancied she saw Spirits. She had knowledge of Old Customs, handed down. She told me about the Witch and the Water in a most charming way, and earnestly believed it.' " He almost shouted, as if she were far away upon a distant summit – which of course she was.

Rain lashed against the casement windows. Wind made strange noises in the chimney. There was a noise outside like the sea as the doctor dipped into the book here and there, skimming, finding anecdotes which related to the woman, casting quick glances over the top of his half-moon glasses for any reaction.

"This is all jolly interesting," he enthused, meaning the book and Rosie, but Rosie said nothing, she had turned to stone. Like one of those monolith-cum-gateposts that Grahl had once leant upon. Rosie of the great and enduring passion, rooted in the land, reduced to a series of anecdotes.

"Can I borrow this?" he shouted. "I'll bring it back next week."

"Keep it," she muttered, and with the exception of a few isolated outbursts in her sleep or frenzies, these were more or less the last words of any sense that anyone in officialdom heard until her 100th year.

* * * * * * *

"She's starting to speak," said the Manager of the Home. "Considering how little use her voice box has had over the years it's surprisingly clear. She talks to herself in the room when she thinks no-one is listening. She's certainly not deaf," he added, fiddling with the underwiring of his bra. Before long he would become a legal 'she' and dress appropriately. Until then his loyal and devoted staff were surprisingly acceptant of the firm upthrust of his breasts beneath his shirt and tie.

Others in the emergency meeting nodded, some more fiercely than others. Some of them, in fact, had been up all night in company with the Wiltshire Fire Brigade, getting residents out of rooms, getting them to shelter in the various utility buildings around the grounds while the office and its records blazed into the clear sky, sending up huge yellow tongues that licked obscenely at the moon as fragments of burning paper, each one depicting portions of a life, were wafted up to the Pleiades to be reborn. During it all they couldn't help but notice that Rosie Chant stood before the inferno like some priestess of the Moonfires, covered in ash, consumed within her own ecstasies.

A weak sun now slid across the windows, spreading over the flat mood of their meeting like margarine. Winsley Hill glistened in the distance and a small white minibus toiled up its steep road: by a freak of wind they could hear the grinding of its gears.

Eleanor Brittle, sensing the drift, was determined to speak out on Rosie's behalf.

"Look, I think we should address one simple fact before we consider any punitive measures. We don't *know* she was responsible for the fire."

"No-one wants to punish her," said her key-worker, Mrs Bennet – she of the hirsute legs and oniony smell. "But is she right for this place? We are hardly geared up for her sort of behaviour. She's spent a lifetime in a mental hospital and we are, in any case, under-staffed. We don't have enough Grade 'A' nurses to do the real work."

"Er … at the moment, anyway," said the Manager, who in his former life had been a chartered accountant and who was now ruling the Home like a kind of Great He/She whose decisions were necessarily infallible, and who had awful powers over what destinies remained to his clients.

"All right, at the moment," conceded the key-worker sharply. "But even so I cannot see how she can stay here. We can't cope. There's too many chiefs and not enough indians. The other residents are afraid of her. She is showing more and more signs of aggression."

"Well wouldn't you?" came Eleanor, her new-found champion, fiddling with her mood rings. "After all that time in a mental hospital? She's 100 years old for God's sake!"

"But is she?" asked the Manager pondering, as Managers do when they're not dreaming of surgical castration. "She doesn't look it. And no-one ever found anything in her records to confirm. It could have been a typing error. She won't tell us anything that makes sense."

"Can the hospital confirm?" asked an anonymous social worker attached to the Home, inured to such internecine warfare and the hidden agendas which lay beneath the surface like anti-personnel mines.

"No, her records were destroyed in a fire donkeys years ago – but blame the Luftwaffe for that one!"

Faces were pulled, there was token laughter from some. The room was full of grey clouds and the stink of old smoke. *She must go* someone seemed to say. But where?

✳ ✳ ✳ ✳ ✳ ✳ ✳

Skraaaa said the crows, in the last days of that summer in 1908, and Rosie in the Old Tea Rooms looked out of the window and saw them on the lawn, black and tattered priests on the neat grass, celebrating their own bloody communion with a worm. The room was full as Grahl held court, unbowed by his encounter with Sir Charles, and with his warm voice and personable manner, his tousled blond hair and light summer clothes, he was like some modern sun-god bringing a new dispensation to the moon-people on the hill.

"But you will allow, sir," he said, "that if your scholar in northern England can identify Wensley and Thorley as references to Woden and Thor, then it is not unreasonable to accept Winsley and Turleigh as likewise?"

The throng marvelled: that an American should know so much about their little world! Some of them, judging from their faces, seemed to reason that if God knew everything about falling sparrows, then Grahl's lesser omniscience was not so unexpected.

"After all, this plateau is littered with names like Danes Bottom, Dane Lee. Dane Hollow and the like."

"Well," said Denham, a bespectacled young man with crinkled hair who fancied himself as a radical, "King Alfred has always been said to have fought the Danes here. That would explain it, of course. So it's 'Woden's Ley' rather than 'Winae's Ley'. Rather nice, that."

Cups rattled in saucers, agreements were muttered. There was a smell of coffee in the air which was completely alien and vaguely repugnant to some of them.

"On the other hand," said the host's wife, interrupting this mood of marvel, "there is always the possibility that the local use of 'Dane' is a corruption of the much older name 'Dôn', wife of the old Celtic deity Bel. Look at Belcombe in Bradford. Bel's Hill. Bel and Dôn. Dôn Rise. Dôn's Lea ..."

It was more interjection than argument. She didn't like Grahl, or what she saw as her husband's unhealthy fascination for the golden outsider. She didn't like Rosie Chant, either, and the way she was getting above herself. She could remember when she had paid Rosie to clean for her, yet here she was now, a sort of guest of honour.

Rosie sat politely, uneasy. She heard the crows again and thought she saw Charlie walk past, his silly hat bobbing over the hedgerow. He seemed to be everywhere, these days.

"Well there is that too," said the American to his hostess, generously enough, pausing to light a cigarette and blow smoke to the ceiling before continuing. "But, anyhow, my intention here today is to explain to you one of the sources of my knowledge and research, which – though I say it who shouldn't – is unique."

His magnetism was in full flow. Almost every person in that room seemed to feel that he addressed them and them alone, and even the Macleod sisters perched in the window seat controlled their giggles and took on a certain gravity as they listened. It was something to do with his voice, his eyes. Nothing anyone could identify for certain.

"Now many of you will have seen me a-walking with Miss Chant, and drawn your own inferences. But let me say now, publicly, my intentions have been entirely pure!"

He smiled gorgeously, the people laughed. There must have been two dozen of them crammed into that room, with several of the younger men lolling on the open staircase. Rosie looked at the floor and blushed. She could almost see the blush in her brand new patent leather shoes. *Was it true?* she thought, her heart plummeting, her mind tugging at the words until they were as bloody and sliced as the worm outside. Well, she wished the earth would swallow her up, although in truth it had done so the moment she had been born.

"Some of you, I know, have been to the Theosophical Society in Bath, and one of the Spiritualist churches, so you have some understanding of the mind's peculiar powers. So with the aid of Miss Chant's wonderful psychometry and sensitivity I have been able to unlock the secrets of this one hill, and I intend – in my thesis – to use this as a small model of the ancient Celtic world as a whole. Sometimes scholarship can get in the way of real vision. And yes, Mrs Denham, I will agree with you that 'Dane' is more probably a corruption of 'Dôn' …"

Rosie stopped listening. She put the slight out of her mind. She had her *I'm going to teach them* air about her, and she determined to prove certain things to them all. If she didn't, she would let Grahl down badly and undermine his whole important work on Winsley Hill. Especially now that he had, unaccountably, fallen foul of Sir Charles and that circle on the very summit of the multi-layered yet invisible sacred mountain on which the English classes lived.

Grahl read from his notes. They were transcriptions of some of the things that Rosie had seen, in vision, amid the stones of No Man's Land. He finished reading with a sort of flourish, a *tra-la!* in his voice as if it were all unchallengeable.

"I must challenge this," said Mrs Denham, ignoring her husband's venomous glance. "I mean I don't doubt that Miss Chant here" – and she pointedly didn't look at Rosie – "actually *saw* something about the women and the snail shells and the people bringing salt. But how do we know it's accurate? I can see things, or imagine them. Anyone can."

Grahl smiled his sun-god smile, perfect teeth and dimples. Rosie shifted her weight in the chair and took a deep breath. She did things within her head, at the back of her mind, which she couldn't explain or teach, but which came easily nonetheless. She was ready for this.

"A volunteer please," said Grahl. "You sir? Would you be so kind as to give, say, that watch to Miss Chant to hold for a little while?"

The old man, Harkes, a small plump and retired baker, undid the watch from its chain and handed it over, leaning forward with his elbows on his knees, determined not to miss a thing. Chairs screeked as people turned to look. Only a couple of them had been to the Theosophical Society and the Spiritualist Church: the rest had not the slightest idea what psychometry was, or what Miss Chant's 'special talents' involved. Silence descended, and seemed to impact around Rosie who sat quietly with the watch in her hands, turning it to and fro, lost in thought. Lost in thought. Lost in thought and spirit on Winsley Hill.

And then she told him things. Slowly at first but with increasing confidence. She told him about his long-dead mother and father and two aunts, and himself as a boy, and the collie with no tail, and the girl with golden tresses that he lost to the fever. And she told him about the clock in his hall, and the fall from a horse, and the pain in his hip and the nephew at sea with the crooked teeth. She told him – ah, lots of things that would be trivial to us or in the telling, but which touched him like kisses and made him fight the tears.

"That's all," she said, and handed him back the watch; and it wasn't little nothing farmhand Rosie Chant who sat there now but a priestess in her power, secure within her Mystery.

"Thank you," said Mr Harkes softly, wiping at his eyes with a large handkerchief. "Thank you very much." And for long seconds that was all that was said, for people were impressed, moved, excited beyond words, terrified.

"Now Mrs Denham what do you think?" The clock ticked loudly in the room and the woman all but glared at Grahl. She hated the man and hated her husband's *I-told-you-so* smirk.

"Look … there are other explanations."

"No," said the old man, quite sharply, eyes red and moist. "No, Mary Denham, I believe it, I do. That young lady there told me things that no-one could have known. And I thank her, with all of my heart, for bringing me that word from my beloved. That one word which has now made the past few years worthwhile after all." He couldn't talk. Tears now poured down his cheeks, and people reached over to touch his shoulders in comfort. Rosie, eyes fixed modestly to the floor, glowed with the pride of Lucifer.

Although Mrs Denham believed in such things completely, and would have crowed about them from the rooftops had it been anyone other than Grahl involved, she wouldn't surrender. Her two guests brought out the worst in her.

"Even so –" she started, with the voice of scientific reason, but Grahl was ready for her.

"But now why not test her yourself? If you would kindly remove, say, that rather fine necklace and give it to Miss Chant?"

Well, as the rest of them said later, Mary looked as if she wanted to fall through the floor. And if they had marked psychism themselves, or better still were in touch with select gossip, they would have known about that necklace and her married lover, and the secret trysts at Tellisford and her second-best husband with his strange tastes and predilection for pain.

"Please?" he said, and looked at her and nodded to the necklace as if in taunt.

He knows, thought Mary Denham with an inner snarl. She went white; she felt dreadful.

"Please leave," she said in a quiet voice. And because people either hadn't heard, or hadn't believed what they heard, she said again louder: "All of you. Please leave. Get out of here."

Her guests were bewildered. They looked at her and then Grahl and then Mr Denham. It was clear to all of them that there were things going on below the surface that they couldn't quite see. The husband said nothing, but stared at her with open disgust. Without another word they all got up and filed silently out, leaving the two parts of the marriage wriggling like the severed ends of the crows' worm.

* * * * * * *

At dusk, where three roads meet, going through the stone circle on her way home, still thrumming with the power of vision and Grahl's parting words: "Soon, Rosie, I want you to hold the Luck. The Luck of the hill. I want you to hold the Luck for me and see where it takes us. That's the most important thing of all."

Soon, he had said. And she chewed upon this in the same way that a later generation would chew upon GI gum.

Footsteps in the road. The shy, bright face of Charlie Kellaway, his hat meticulous on his brow, his collar immaculate and tie well-knotted. Rosie tutted and looked him up, and looked him down. She wasn't mere Rosie Chant just then: if Sir Charles held keys to the valley, then she held sway upon the heights. A side of her knew that just then. A side of her had always known it.

Go away she thought toward Charlie, mere farmhand that he was, in his silly hat and old boots.

"Rosie ..." he said, and you could almost hear his heart pounding, for in his mind there were destinies at stake just then, between this world and the next; while that scaly consciousness within the hill, beneath their feet and sealed within its cavern, blinked its ancient eyes and held its breath.

"Will ye be coming to the dance with me next week?" he blurted out, his voice rather higher than usual, his words running into each other. The low clouds behind Rosie were turned into strange scarlet landscapes by the setting sun. Hills, lakes and weird horizons rolled and broiled beyond her head and showed portents of her true realm. And the old, old consciousness within Charlie and beneath his feet knew that he used more nerve in that request in the middle of No Man's Land on Winsley Hill than he ever would within another No Man's Land in Flanders, where the Kaiser's artillery ripped him as badly as Rosie was about to do.

"Me?" she said, looking up with a light in her eye that he was afraid to interpret. The clouds behind her rolled and tumbled over Farleigh Wick and took on the colours of spilled royal blood. Nations within the sky and man's future clashed and changed shape as he waited. "What ... *me?*"

Swallowing hard, Charlie nodded. He took off his hat, wiped his brow with a perfectly ironed piece of cloth and replaced the hat as precisely as before, his fingers flexing, the back of his knees trembling.

"Charlie ..." she said, touching his shoulder very lightly, smiling gently, gathering her words in order to blast and lacerate him in the way that made the Chants locally famous. "Charlie, I thought I told you —"

Skraaaaa! came a single crow behind her, and she turned and saw the low and murderous tumult on the horizon, and there was enough of the sybil in her then as to have some portent of the boy's own likely fate, in a far-off land among the dead and dying. She had glimpses of … oh, terrible things, and the malice went from within her. "Oh Charlie go home please. Not another word, just go home will you?"

So Charlie did.

She loves me he thought. He was almost certain.

But it wasn't love, or goodness, which turned her words that moment. Rosie, who was destined to lose her child and the rest of her own life, had just glimpsed the loss of a whole generation.

* * * * * * *

"You're the talk of the Lanes," said Maggie Chant when she had stopped coughing. Logs crackled, sparks rose in the narrow chimney. Their faces were two pale blobs at either end of the dark and draughty room.

"You want to stop smoking that pipe. Cigarettes are much better for you. Mr Grahl smokes a special sort that's specially designed for athletes – runners, that sort."

"You're the talk of the Lanes," said the mother again, spitting in a large tin that she kept by her bed that once held Cherry Blossom boot polish.

"That's disgusting," said Rosie untouchable and untouched.

"Aye but it's true. I don't know who you are any more."

They heard a vixen outside, yowling, so much like a woman in pain. They heard a badger snuffling and snorting across their plot and dogs yelping on the distant farm, and loud voices (carried a freakish distance) from the *Fox and Hounds* at Farleigh Wick. And Rosie couldn't sleep, the room was filled with her spirits, with crossed destinies and potentials. She didn't know who she was either. Not the old Rosie Chant, that was for sure.

"Stop spitting mother will you? It's just become a habit."

And she turned her face to the cool wall and smiled.

* * * * * * *

In 1990 Mrs Bennet resigned from the Home and started a new job at Bowyers. At her interview, freshly depilated and deodorised, she was impressed by the fact that they were not interested in certificates or qualifications. Someone with her drive and attitude, they inferred, could become very big in pies in the years to come.

So Rosie got herself a new key-worker and a champion at last in the shape of Eleanor Brittle who had been just aching to have this chance.

Eleanor, who threw herself into her communication courses in a manic urge to better herself and help the world, had craved this challenge. She had also been celibate for months, which was not entirely unconnected. Her former boyfriend Darrel, who had his own Hometune business, swore that once she started improving her interpersonal skills, as she called them, she lost all talent for shagging. And considering that, well, he could have any woman in Trowbridge if he so much as flashed his strobe light, there wasn't much point in them going out any more was there?

None of this mattered to Rosie. As far as she was concerned all these key-workers, nurses, social workers, therapists and the like tended to fade into one another over the decades and become indistinguishable, as did the carpets, curtains and bed-pans. To Rosie, Eleanor Brittle was no more than a small presence who wore ylang-ylang perfume, crystal pendants, and shone her ambition around like a torch.

"She has so much potential!" said Eleanor with the energy and passion of youth, although she was nearly 30 and no longer as young as she acted.

"She is also very old," said the Manager, quietly smug and almost happy now that the insurance aspects of the recent fire had been sorted out (quite advantageously) and with a minimum of fuss. And even more happy now that the date for the creation of his vagina had been confirmed.

"So what kind of ageist comment is that?" came Miss Brittle, determined to hold her ground.

The review committee around the great oval table nodded. They were always vaguely supportive as a group but rarely had any clear idea as to whom or what they were being supportive. Eleanor Brittle, who had little personality but ample political correctness to fill that void, could be dangerous in such situations, in this day and age.

"But once again," she persisted, "how old is she, exactly? I can't find anything to show that's she's much older than, say, 80 – or perhaps 83 at the most. She looks about that age doesn't she? Compared to other residents that we're sure about? So let's say that she was born around, oh, 1910. Somewhere near Devizes. Probably the illegitimate child of a farm worker who was taken away from the scandal. If we can project onto her some sort of personalised, historicised image – however awry – then we can come closer to respecting and empathising with her individuality.

We can treat her as a whole person with unique integrity rather than just a blank slate ..."

On and on, on and on ... you couldn't help but sympathise with Darrel when she got like this. In 1908 even the most learned would have understood very little of what she said. In 1990 not a great deal had changed. Yet at a stroke Eleanor had, on levels of poetry and metaphor, given back to Rosie some two decades of her life.

"We know that she is becoming increasingly vocal. Her speech is so good that I cannot believe she is deaf at all."

The anonymous social worker, who sat in the corner and cultivated her anonymity as a kind of self-defence, fiddled with her filofax and shifted uneasily. There would be a request for money soon, she just knew it. The recent austerity years had given her finely tuned senses in that respect.

"What I'm suggesting then, is that we contact Dr McHaffee in Devizes to discuss her case, find some funding to pay for complete assessments by both Speech and Hearing Therapists from St Martin's Hospital, plus regular sessions in Recall Therapy which I'll organise myself, and a daily plan of actualisation which —"

There were screams from downstairs, the sound of breaking glass. Then the sound of sensible shoes hurrying down the polished wooden staircase that only staff could use. The Manager made a quick internal phone call.

"It seems, Eleanor, that your blank slate has just actualised her potential by head-butting the picture window. There's blood all over the place, apparently. You wouldn't want to take her to Bradford hospital would you?"

*   *   *   *   *   *   *

Rosie sat with her head swathed in bandages, in the back of Eleanor's muddy-brown Montego. She had Sister Ndlovu as an escort, who was a real 'Scale C' nurse that they called upon when they were especially short-staffed. Swathed in bandages, swathed in dreams, she escorted her own memories up Winsley Hill for the first time in over 80 years. She knew the place and yet she didn't. She failed to recognise much and yet she recognised it all, in essence. Under the railway bridge, over the canal and then the river. **WINSLEY** said the sign on the lower slopes, the car changing down a gear to cope.

Rosie's heart beat fast, half-expecting at any moment, somehow, to see The Man again just as she had left him, striding up the hill with his hands behind his back. She hardly dared blink as they overtook some mountain bikes toiling upward; slowed for two young women on horseback ambling contemptuously down; and changed gears within herself as her memory sought to connect with the changes that had been made upon the hill by progress and a thirst for property.

"Oh my ... she's crying," said Sister Ndlovu, holding Rosie's hand in the back seat.

"I expect it hurt!" said Eleanor, overtaking a tractor, speeding up and then slowing down, past the signs at the west of the village saying **BYPASS NOW!** and then going slower still to manoeuvre the narrow twisting road that snaked through the old part of the village. Here at least, the grey high walls hadn't changed much in 100 years. And when she saw the griffins flanking the gates of what would be the new hospice, it all suddenly came into focus like the separate scenes in a child's Viewmaster, jiggled into 3-D.

"Ooh!" said the escort sharply as Rosie's nails dug into her hand, though without malice. Eleanor glanced into her mirror, at the mummified head and the intensely-alive eyes. She had been on two courses for Challenging Behaviour and knew what to do. "That's a hospice, Rose," she said in an understanding tone that was non-threatening and respectful. "Don't worry, you won't be going there!" she breezed, for humour was also a useful technique in such situations.

But Rosie had been in that building before in the years before she was now, officially, said to have been born. She had been there when the nights had started to draw in, and frost covered the whole valley below, and she had sat before a crowd and held the Luck against her better judgement and felt her whole life start to fall apart. She turned to watch the griffins until the car went around the corner past the *Seven Stars*. She wondered who had chiselled their willies off. Wouldn't have happened in her day.

NO BYPASS! said a new set of signs at the eastern edge of the village before it gave way, briefly, to open fields at either side.

"Luck," she said out loud, and the youngsters sat up and looked but couldn't see anything.

Oh God there's so much potential here! thought Eleanor again, like a prayer of thanks.

CHAPTER FIVE

If the chronicles of old light on Winsley Hill were ever dragged up from the caverns beneath and dusted down, and then scanned and edited by that Power which rules its lanes and levels, the end product would have to include Rosie's final glimpse of the last Winsley Wheeler as he made his frantic circuit round Conkwell, Haugh and the Ashleys, plucking at his bell and thus smiting (as he fancied) all his opponents into the dust of the track.

If these chronicles were given any footnotes then this incident alone would have an asterisk and a sentence saying: *Summer ended here; the days grew shorter.*

Wrrrrrrrh! he'd snarl to anyone who'd catch his eye, waving and shaking his fist in defiance, hatless and collarless and sleeves rolled up, with his blond curls plastered onto his brow by the sweat of many miles, and the wild red eyes of thwarted youth. Once he had been a leader, now he was a loner. With that outbreak of cattle and horse mutilation which continued through the summer, and the public loathing which jabbed like an accusing finger at every likely candidate, he was the only Wheeler who had not turned his bicycle into a ploughshare, a worthy cause, or doting wife. So he cycled the old routes like the Flying Dutchman does the sea-lanes, plucking at his bell and high on either cider or gin depending on the time of day. Yet deprived of the group, his *wrrrrrrrh!* had no power, his wheels no direction.

The chronicles would show on that day how Rosie, in her old clothes, was back among the mortals again and fixing one of the walls near her house which drunken revellers had knocked down rather than use the nearby stile. Rosie-in-the-Lanes where she really belonged, watching the insect life between the stones scuttle round beneath her gaze: bursts of white spiders, ribbons of translucent centipedes, clusters of ladybirds and wood lice. She crushed them all.

Wrrrrrrh! she heard from behind, and there was the Last Wheeler, standing on his pedals, swaying the bicycle from side to side as though he forged up a steep hill when it was only the flat road from Little Ashley. She ignored him and lifted another stone from the mess that was scattered over the lane. Earth and wood lice fell from the bottom and down her dress; one of the creatures popped beneath her fingers.

"You'll have to wait," she snapped and turned back to her work, damned sure she wasn't going to clear a way through specially for him.

"I don't wait for no-one," he snarled back, getting off the bike and bouncing it across the debris with one hand and pushing Rosie out of the way and into the ditch with the other. "Least of all a Yankee's shag-bag like you!"

And if those chronicles of old light on Winsley Hill could be received in volume as well as vision, then you would hear the dragon in the caverns beneath sucking its breath over its yellow fangs and go *Oooooh!* For you didn't say things like that to one of the Chants.

"You shouldn't have said that," said Rosie, calmly enough, but getting a better grip on the stone. The young man stopped and turned, sneering as he re-mounted his machine, not appreciating the danger he was in. But then again he wasn't from the hill itself. He – rebel and dangerous character that he was – lived with his mum and dad in Broughton Gifford, and had a cat named Dimple.

Now Maggie Chant would have just ripped him apart with her tongue, completely humiliated the wretch, and no-one would have seen him around the Lanes again. But Rosie didn't have her mother's generosity of spirit.

"I'll say what I want!" he told her, turning his bike to face her, both feet on the ground, speaking to her as he always did to his parents.

Rosie's manner changed.

"Oh look ..." she said softly. "Look I'm sorry. Come here. No no ... come here." And there was an air about her movements, a tone about her voice which made it seem as if the Yankee's shag-bag might be about to become a Broughton-Giffordian's shag-bag. Which was all he ever wanted in life anyway.

"I'll just put this down," she said, her eyes glinting in clear lust, looking for a place to put the flat, grey stone. The work of her grandfathers, whose spirits were even then nagging her on psychic and genetic levels to finish the task, could wait a bit longer. The proper relations between Man and Woman and the Order of Things on Winsley Hill came first.

"Right," he muttered, swallowing hard, and even if she was a bit of a dog he wanted her anyway. That was what being a Wheeler was all about. Anything to lose his virginity. He swallowed again and gripped his handlebars and couldn't believe his luck. Luck? He was terrified.

Rosie half-turned away and swung the heavy stone toward the wall yet didn't release it, so that the momentum carried her arms back around in a graceful arc that came smashing down upon his left hand. The last of the Wheelers screamed, fell from his bike, pushed his bleeding hand under his right armpit, staggered onto his feet and used his good hand to fend off another blow which glanced off the side of his head.

"Christ!" he cried, grabbing his precious bike and backing away down the lane, biting back the sobs, before leaping onto the saddle and pedalling off one-handed with even less balance but greater speed than ever before.

"Go to buggery!" she yelled, taking up a fist-sized lump of stone and hurling it after him, catching him square between the shoulder-blades so that he arched back in pain and almost came off.

Yankee shag-bag? She fumed.

"I hope you die!" she shouted to the disappearing figure. "I hope you bloody well die!"

Fuming, raging, taking deep breaths, she started on the wall again. The depredations of the age and its lack of discipline, the ill work of the rebelsome drunken youth was made good again as each stone was fitted roughly where it had gone before. The spirits of the grandfathers – never too concerned with daily issues of life and death and loving – were considerably mollified now that their wall was fixed. *Thank ye very much!* they seemed to say, and sat on the wall with their pipes smoking furiously, pulling hard on their astral tobacco, the bliss of the afterlife matched only by their memories of rightness and Old Holborn.

And as for Rosie …

"Wrrrrrrh …" she muttered. "I'll give him bloody wrrrrrrrrh …"

* * * * * * *

Evening. Mother and daughter on the old bench propped against their house, looking across the empty fields and the swallows wheeling in the sky, ready to leave for winter. The stone wall at the back released its latent heat, the sun warmed their faces and all was well, and all was very well between them on the hill. They sipped tea from big tin mugs and slurped a lot. Mother and daughter, in the evening of their relationship, had somehow met again across an emptiness, and released warmth toward each other.

Maggie Chant was humming. An old song whose words she couldn't quite remember but which her mother had sung to her as a child. Maggie Chant had thought a lot about her mother lately, and often felt her presence during the lonely hours when the pain came and the coughing. She sometimes glimpsed her old dad, too, and thought she'd seen him near the wall that afternoon, inspecting it as he often did during his lifetime. The swallows drew a massive curve in the violet sky and flew off south, to another world beyond all Maggie's imagining. *Time to go* she thought.

Rosie touched her mother's hand, on an impulse of affection.

"I'm sorry mum," she said, suddenly noticing how gaunt the other looked. "I mean –"

"I know what you mean," said her mother, clasping Rosie's hand with hers so that they sat there in silence, creatures of the dusk and earth, marvelling at the bright star and the crescent moon both low in the bare sky, and the manic flittering of bats above their thatch.

"You'll be gone from me soon," said Maggie softly, squeezing hard, remembering the plump little girl she had once held in her lap, and whom she could protect from all evil with all the strength in the world. She sighed, and adjusted the red silk ribbon she wore in her hair, shaded her eyes from the low sun. In truth she had stopped worrying about her daughter and Grahl. The money had been a godsend after all: an arrangement between destinies for her daughter's deliverance. A bell sounded across the fields, tolling in time with her heart. What will be, will be, on Winsley Hill. And then she almost remembered the words of that song: something about women and corn, and fat babbies, and men coming home.

Rosie kept quiet. The moment was too good to spoil with discussion. She was just pleased to see her mother sober again, with her best blue dress and something done with her hair. Things were for the best, she'd see. And then she took up the tune instead, humming and *la-la-ing* it, trawling for the words and then hauling them up in memory's net so that the whole tune burst to the surface all silver, alive and bubbling. And they were like sisters, beating time in the air, swaying from side to side on the rickety bench, beyond time and pure in their love. And that was the best they'd known, or would ever know, when they sang together upon the hill, at the dusk, as the leaves began to fall.

"Ooh," said Maggie, as they linked arms and laughed. "What'll folk think of us?"

"Who cares?" said Rosie Chant. "Who will ever care?"

* * * * * * *

It was the Kellaways who broke the spell, a whole gang of them, flowing up their track like a swarm of hornets, all hats and shadows, boots, sticks and attitudes, with young Charlie following behind – a lantern of embarrassment.

"They would!" said Maggie sharply as the group stopped and their leader came forward.

"Margaret," he said curtly, touching the brim of his old bowler.

"Albert," she replied, without inflexion.

"There's been another slicing. That little foal down Turner's field? The black 'un? Well it were cut up summat awful …"

The two women said nothing in the brief silence that followed. They were sharing the horror.

"We 'ad to kill 'er."

"Felt sick, I did."

"The blood …"

"Some bastard'll pay for this!"

"Its poor eyes …"

They all spoke at once. Used to death, and matter-of-fact in their own treatment of animals, they were appalled by this. Flogging a lazy horse was one thing; kicking your pigs was another; but what had been done to the foal made their flesh creep. It wasn't natural. They didn't know what the world was coming to. Kellaways and Chants, enemies for centuries, were united for once, and it took butchery to do it.

"We found this near, in the ditch. Here Jim, show 'er."

The man held up a large clasp knife, covered in blood. There was no such thing as fingerprinting in those days, or concern about AIDS or hepatitis: he grasped it in his hand as firmly as the attacker would have done.

"So what you make of this then, Rosie? Eh?" and Albert took the knife and passed it to her, and some of them knew exactly why he did, for they had grown up around rumours or actual experience of her strange talents. And because the Age of Reason had never quite touched down upon their class as they worked the land, they believed it without question even if they couldn't – or daren't – say much out loud. The word 'witch' had fierce echoes in all their vocabularies.

All eyes jabbed on Rosie. Eyes which had done nothing more than scorn her womanhood as much as they feared her powers. *Yankee shag-bag* she thought, and it was what they all thought upon the hill, she supposed, and she had an image of the Wheeler and his hateful face. A meteor scratched its mark upon the darkening sky. The tolling bell stopped.

"Did ye see anyone Rosie?" asked Albert. "Only them police are no damn good to anyone. We're pretty desp'rate. Did ye see anyone who might ha' done this? Used this?"

Yankee shag-bag she thought again.

"I saw one o' them Wheelers," she said, not knowing it was the Last of the Wheelers. "He had —"

"I know the one!" cried someone, and he described the man exactly, naming him even, and it was as if each one burst into flame and crackled loudly.

"He's from *Brough*-ton *Giff*-ord!" someone else said, dissecting the words in disgust, as if this explained everything, every depredation under the sun.

"Right then lads, we'll be getting about our business and reporting this to the constabulary as law-abiding folk do."

But they all knew what Albert meant by that. They turned and strode off, pushing Charlie out of the way as he stood, heart a-fluttering, and tried to make eye-contact with Rosie.

"Margaret," he said again, though less curtly, touching the brim once more.

"Albert."

"You haven't seen us."

"Never 'ave, never will."

He nodded; they understood each other perfectly.

"You'll be wanting this," said Rosie, handing back the knife after closing its blade into the handle, lifting the hem of her dress to wipe her hand. A flash of leg which Charlie and Albert couldn't fail to notice.

"Thanking you," said the latter, who turned and strode away, pushing the younger man before him.

"Good riddance," said Maggie, when he was still in earshot, unable to resist a last bit of venom. And then: "Rosie … did ye really see that Wheeler?"

The daughter nodded.

"No, I mean when you held the knife. Did you *see* him?"

Rosie shrugged. "Who cares, who ever cares?" she repeated, but the earlier mood had long gone, and the chronicles of old light on Winsley Hill turned to a new and darker chapter from then on.

* * * * * * *

Another gale ripped down the valley, smashing at the Home, loosening tiles, making doors slam and curtains flutter; and every garden fence that wasn't east-west aligned was pushed flat. And the gulley in which the Home stood caught the wind like the sucked-in cheeks of a child and made strange moaning, shrieks, and muted howls.

"Rose, I want you to meet two ladies, Misses Straffon and Pryce. They are Speech and Hearing Therapists!" Eleanor, who had started a course on basic sign language at Bath College, and bought two illustrated 'Sign and Say' books to build up her vocabulary, spoke awkwardly, with strange rhythms as she tried to sign and fingerspell simultaneously. She was determined to – as she saw it – Communicate. In her mind's ear that word was always capitalised. It was the key to locked gates, was Communication.

Rosie imperiously raised one eyebrow, looked at the blowing curtains in her room, and then back to her visitors who stood there like Three Wise Women awkward before this Mystery. She did indeed use sign language. A deaf girl in the same ward had taught it to her almost 80 years before in the Wiltshire County Asylum, Devizes, where she had had two relationships that were deep and meaningful, as we would say today.

The first was with a woman known loudly to the staff as Deaf Dot, or Daft Deaf Dot as the alliteration and inventiveness took them, she with the large, dimpled body covered by smocks, and hair which stayed like satin even though she never washed it, and her odd moods and even odder glottal noises which also earned her the description 'dumb'. Dot in her dumbness, signing away through the miseries Rosie felt, was as much an outcast as she was. Rosie would braid and brush her long hair and stroke her brow (which Dot liked), and sniffed the woman's hair and skin which smelled so much like a baby's skin that she herself could become exceedingly troubled for reasons she could never explain. Together they made long journeys (of differing sorts and differing ways) without ever leaving the grounds. For 15 years she used nothing else but sign language, and when her friend died of a heart attack Rosie wept.

Centuries later, when the Asylum looked to its semantics and became the Wiltshire County Mental Hospital without any other change but a re-chiselled name on the gates, she was startled one night when a young and shorn-headed woman slipped into her bed and wrapped her bony legs around her. This patient was new, a semi-nocturnal and self-mutilating orphan who simply wanted to snuggle under Rosie's covers, put her head against Rosie's breast and beg for stories. That first night she demanded this with such passion that Rosie felt afraid, and so after much swallowing and many glottal noises herself, she got her voice-box working again, and whispered the first things that came to mind …

Such visits became welcome and indeed much needed. The girl was such an empty vessel that it seemed a way to leech herself a soul: while Rosie in her turn was so bursting full of stories, mythologies, visions, legends and yarns that the pair were almost made for each other, and the cool, bare flesh against hers a source of comfort rather than desire. The chance to whisper in the night, and tell all manner of strange things to an uncritical ear. One gave, the other received; one pushed out, the other drew in. There was no sex, but it doesn't mean that sex was not involved. And the younger woman was eventually taken away – discharged, they called it – before Rosie learned if anything came of such a union. It went on for two years in fact, and Rosie never learnt much about the girl other than her name, which wasn't offered until after the first month: "Marcy Macleod — of the Black Macleods" she said, as if there was some joke or scandal which everyone knew.

Rosie blinked, drew back and looked, had one of her flashes and smiled bright as the Moon though said nothing. *I knew your grandmothers* she thought, as the early sparrows fought and twittered on the lawns.

Rosie's body spent decades in the hospital yet what happened in it before, between, and after those two relationships meant nothing to her. And although her essence never left Winsley Hill during all that time, yet Dot and Marcy led her into hidden places, secret and brief sanctuaries which stopped her going over into madness entirely.

"Hello Rose!" said Misses Straffon and Pryce, one slightly after the other in their practised double-act, both with the sort of hopeful and non-threatening briskness that their job entailed. They were both small, with the sort of dark-and-comely, fair-and-goodly features which could give Popes troilist fantasies – although nothing was in their minds much beyond flip-charts, language schemes, lip-patterns and audiograms. Rosie smiled, the curtains billowed as if from a draught, and when she made a delicate wafting gesture with both hands (meaning 'Welcome!') it was as if the breeze came from her. Miss Straffon the Speech Therapist talked non-stop, causing Eleanor great problems in trying to sign it all. Miss Pryce, with state-of-the-art hearing aids in both ears, each with delicate pink and unobtrusive mouldings that made them look like art-deco jewellery, listened very carefully and soberly, and fiddled with a small case full of sophisticated equipment.

"Just leave us," said one to Eleanor. "We won't take long," said the other. And Eleanor reluctantly left. She wanted to see their secrets, not least because they made her feel so gauche. After all, mood rings, crystal pendants and a right-on attitude were no match for designer clothes and a portable sonar. They were almost professional incarnations of her own burning (though essentially amateurish) desire to Communicate.

"You won't scratch us, will you Rosie?" Miss Straffon whispered, conspiratorially, signing it far more fluently than Eleanor ever could.

Rosie, still in her nightie and slippers, smiled and shook both her head and one fist as a token of 'No!'

* * * * * * *

"So she's not deaf at all?" said the Manager.

"Not at all. Not to any degree," replied Eleanor in a half-triumphant way, though stopping short of using her *I told you so* face. She was no longer NHS, after all. A carrier bag labelled 'Budgens' was blown against the window and the glass rattled as it stuck there for a moment before being snatched down by a rogue current to its bio-degradable fate on some juniper bushes.

"Not even hard-of-hearing?"

"Nope."

"Well fuck me."

The Manager looked down over the grey, wind-swept world that had taken so much labour to create: the car-park and drive, littered with broken roof tiles and fragments of fencing which flapped up and down at each gust, and black bags of rubbish which had been blown from their plastic bins and ripped open by foxes in the night, so that the whole area was strewn with those contents that neither man nor beast wanted. On the Manager's desk was a clumsily-written resignation note from the Junior Manager – the one who could only use her left arm because the right was broken. The tone was hysterical. The threat of legal action was raised. Rosie's name had been mentioned several times. The Manager, who harboured dreams of having a firm young body exactly like hers, sighed.

"Now … in collaboration with the Speech and Hearing Therapists, I've worked out a systematic programme of —"

"Does she really need to be here then?" the elder interrupted.

Eleanor looked up from her neat, plastic-backed white files, startled as a deer caught in the headlights. "Pardon?" she said, disbelievingly, although in the back of her mind she had always known to expect this sort of thing from the private sector.

"I mean, if she is so capable then do we really need to feel obliged to keep her here? She has adequate speech, perfect hearing, a fluency in sign language, plenty of personal skills when she wants to use them, excellent health. And, by your own reckoning, she's also young enough to make a new start elsewhere. Somewhere that can meet her needs better than we can."

Eleanor put her files to one side, scarcely able to speak. It was as if all her plans and programmes were suddenly being used against her.

"We can't do that," she said weakly.

A sudden gust, a noise like air howling through a vast skull. The Manager saw a line of tiles on one of the outbuildings ripped up and flung in the air, in sequence, smashing down on Eleanor's already battered Montego, shattering the windscreen and chiselling great marks in the top and bonnet.

"You had better go and see to your car, Eleanor …"

And when the latter glanced out, again in disbelief, she squealed, though the noise was drowned by another gust even stronger, and glass could be heard shattering from unidentified places around the Home.

"Go on … !"

And she went, slamming the door after her.

The Manager stood at the window, one hand on the pane to stop it rattling, watching Eleanor struggle crab-like against the wind and then open her car door only for a gust to catch it and blow it off its hinges altogether, and her onto the gravel with it. *Serves you right* came the cruel thought. The fact is that he – soon to be she – had ceased to care for Rosie. The Manager (who believed in ghosts) blamed that old lady for many things going wrong within the Home: the fire, the flooding; and now it was as if the spirit of Rosie Chant stood at the head of the valley and somehow caused this new gale and all the unease and unsettled relations that only gales can bring. It had never been like this in the beginning, before Rosie came.

"Trust me," the Manager muttered, watching the small people scurrying below to Eleanor's aid. "I'm rarely wrong."

* * * * * * *

Rosie became a slow-worm in the skull's eye-socket, scanning those opened chronicles of old light which told of past, and present, and what might come. She knew – no *knew* – that The Man was out there again, somehow. It was as if she had turned quickly to the last page and snatched a confused glimpse of her ending. She could feel his mind circling, hovering on unseen currents. She writhed within her coils and felt that at any moment he might swoop and take her in his talons, then give her one final soar before the bloody consummation on some bleak summit.

She sat in her chair, in the Home, looking upon the Hill and remembering the last time she had seen him, in the circle at No Man's Land where three roads meet, when the days were drawn short and lines of fallen leaves writhed and rustled around their ankles by the roadside, pushed by the wind. It was cold and glowering. It felt then as if no bird would sing again, as if the world might end at tea-time.

He's leaving me she thought, and knew what the hollowed-out lightning struck tree felt like which she leaned against.

"Heggerty," he said, or she thought he said. "That's what you are." Rosie said nothing. She watched the way he huddled into his long, dark winter coat, the brim of his matching hat pulled down firmly over his brow, tilted against the stiff breeze. "Here … at the three ways. That's where Heggerty always stands to direct dead souls."

Again, she said nothing. It looked as if he'd been drinking again. He swayed slightly.

"Heggerty," he insisted, as if it were important, pointing at her, spelling it to help her understand. "H-e-c-a-t-e. Heggerty. Here, you, these three roads. Past, present and future. You're a marvel Rosie, you really are."

He swayed some more, paused to fumble for his cigarettes and lit one with difficulty, cupping the match against the wind. "Heggerty directs dead souls to the road they deserve. To Tartarus, a walled place of punishment, if you're an enemy of the Gods; to the, ah, Asphodel Meadows for those who are neither – oh excuse me – neither good nor bad. Or the orchards of Elysium where the, ah, the virtuous will enjoy soft breezes!" A cold wind blew through them, presage of winter, and ice which could burn. "Where oh where will you send me Rosie Chant?" And he half-sang it, swaying and conducting himself with a cigarette.

She didn't understand. She didn't care. It was 1908 and she was pregnant and parentless, and her man was about to leave her, and it was her birthday, she was 18.

"Don't leave me," she said, very softly, and it cost her a lot to say that.

Grahl paused. A flicker of guilt passed across his face and gave him what seemed to be a moment's sobriety. The wind upon the trees sprang up and made a roar like the ocean, and she felt that open-gut psychic cold again that made her shiver from head to foot. Two owls glided across the central road to take up another perch, and he turned to follow her glance.

"Ah …" he slurred. "Owls. Heggerty's birds, y'know. They —"

"Don't leave me!" she said again, more urgently now, pulling her own coat tightly around her solar plexus to stop the drain upon her energy, to try and warm up.

His turn to say nothing, but look at the ground. He wasn't as drunk as he wanted to seem.

Tell him you're pregnant said Rosie to herself as the leaves were now blown in little swirls around the three roads; but it was 1908, and such things didn't come easily between two such people in their strange relationship. And she wasn't entirely sure who the father might be anyway.

He looked up, threw down his cigarette; it scored a line in the dusk like a meteor coming to earth.

"Rosie …" he started, and in that split second (analysed a million times in the decades to come) he was not the praeter-human being full of presence and import, nor yet the life-draining incubus with strange powers. Whatever may have overshadowed him in Rosie's vision at least, was briefly banished, and for that instant he was just a young American in his twenties, far from home, who had stirred himself up a whole lot of trouble and now wanted out. "Rosie I —" but the panting and snorting of a horse stopped him as it hauled its carriage up the dark tunnel of the overhanging trees on the middle road from Warleigh.

The driver was so muffled against the cold that only his eyes could be seen under the little peaked cap, eyes that were reddened with hell-fires or conjunctivitis, you couldn't have said which at that moment. The carriage stopped, waited; the horse raised and lowered its hooves in sequence, snorting, keen to be off again. Grahl never finished the sentence. Words which might have altered Rosie's entire life went unsaid, and she knew with certainty that her own road would lead to what he called Tartarus, that walled place of punishment which found shape in the mental hospital at Devizes.

"I have to go, Rosie. No, I have to."

Skraaa skraaa skraaa! came the crows in the darkening day.

Tell him you're pregnant, came the voice. *Tell him you love him.*

"Please stay," she said, and added pathetically: "It's my birthday."

There was the merest hint of a pause from Grahl but no more than that as he climbed into the carriage and tucked the blanket around his legs before slinking down in the seat. The driver flicked at the horse, the carriage rocked and jerked forward. Rosie in the dusk, in despair, the light being sucked from her heart and thus from the world itself, jogging alongside as it gathered pace.

"Please … oh please," as she reached to him, over the wheel.

Grahl sat up suddenly. "Look, just stay there will you?" he urged. "I'll come back. You don't understand. Somehow I'll come back!" And he spoke with more warmth then, as they drew apart, than he had ever done when they walked the Lanes, or when they mated. It was as if the rising dark had brought his guilt, his humanity, up to the surface with it, if only for an instant.

Rosie stopped and watched him go, the carriage growing smaller in the distance.

"Bye," he said faintly, slumping back in the seat and waving backward over his shoulder with the malign sign language of love's disinterest. She could have been an irritating wasp that he tried to flick away. The road curved it out of sight. Suddenly it was finished. She heard the owls screech and Winter began.

CHAPTER SIX

There are places where three roads meet in all of our lives, where Heggerty directs us daily: at the bottom of our brains, at the back of our minds, or just beyond the next hour. Rosie continued to go to these crossroads, and experience that final parting, for almost nine decades afterward. In 1908, when it happened in the flesh, the stone circle was unbroken, the roads were of trodden earth rutted by carts, the dry-stone walls were intact and almost sacred, the trees were more numerous and vied with the humans in their sense of worth upon the hill, and the world still kept some wild innocence. In Rosie's 100th year, when the same event continued to happen in her spirit (though no less tangibly), the circle was scattered, the trees thinned and subdued, the walls had taken on the battered air of rustic novelty and the roads between were metalled … yet Heggerty could still be felt, and the road down to Warleigh could still be imagined as leading toward darkness.

"Please, oh please," said Eleanor, coming toward Rosie up the psychological equivalent of that road, rising toward the old lady's consciousness and hearing. Eleanor continued to use hesitant sign language, despite the report of the hearing therapist. "Please, oh please. Communicate," she begged, as her vegetarian dog gobbled the cat food and made the bowl slide around the floor.

Eleanor was using the Recall pack, projecting photos onto a blank wall, desperately trying to touch some chord. Scenes, people, fashions, vehicles and headlines from the 1930s onward. Stories about royal scandals, airships burning, strange crosses in Germany, hunger marches to London, and gas masks. All of which, Eleanor felt, might touch upon the world that Rosie knew in her young and impressionable twenties.

The button clicked, light spumed, a new scene and headline: *Amelia Earhart lost on Pacific flight*. It meant nothing to Rosie, who would have been 47 years old then, and well shut away and lost herself for nearly three decades. Locked away within her soul, where the three roads perpetually meet.

Eleanor sighed and switched off the projector, then drew the curtains. The low sun made them both blink, and Rosie shield her eyes.

"Rosie, please communicate with me. We've got to help you unlock this potential you have. I sense your anger but we need to help you relate to things. You don't know what might be in store for you otherwise."

She meant *Tigh Aisling*, the home in Bath where there had been so much trouble, and where the Manager wanted to dump Rosie. She meant loss of face for herself. She meant her contract which may not be renewed. She meant …

"I do," said Rosie, and Eleanor gasped, for she had never yet heard this voice which came like a whisper up a long tube.

"I'm sorry? What do you mean?"

Rosie swallowed. After generations of virtual (though not total) silence, her vocal chords were not as they could be. "I … *do* know … what's in store."

Eleanor took a deep breath. Her heart was pounding. She felt that Rosie was coming to meet her at last, instead of endlessly running away. She felt that wheels were beginning to turn. "Please, Rosie … talk to me."

So Rosie took her hand. A touch as light and dry as leaves. And Rosie talked to her. She told her about the babies that she, Eleanor, had miscarried, and the moped she had crashed, and the boyfriend with the limp and bad attitude, and the leather coat she had torn from armpit to hip, and the man in the kitchen that she met in a pub and dreamed about later, guiltily. She told her things, marvellous things, no-one-else-could-know things, and Rosie was back in her power again as she had been in the Old Tea Rooms at Conkwell, and on dozens of other occasions when she had walked on the hill with Grahl.

The younger woman pulled her hand away. Blood was pounding in her head. It was not totally correct but it was almost so. There was a look about Rosie like a young girl saying *I told you so*, and Eleanor knew that the rumours were true. "Oh my God, Rosie, how do you know all this? Where is this all coming from?"

The old lady pointed one gnarled finger to the empty corner of the room, where Eleanor fancied she must have seen some spirit, who told her these things. But in truth she was pointing through walls, beyond the trees, over the valley and toward the mass of the hill where it all began.

"Look Rosie, I'll … I'll see you tomorrow …" and she clipped the lead onto the collar of her sated dog, dragging it out so hard that the beast coughed and wheezed. Still shocked, almost trembling, she hurried out to sit in her car, locked all the doors and shouted at the dog to sit down in the back, which it did after squirling around a ritual three times. The side windows and windscreen of the Montego had been replaced, but all the dents and the seats which had been ripped open by the flying tiles made it feel less like a sanctuary than an old, run-down cinema that she sat inside. Before her the Home towered and menaced like a dinosaur from that film which was all the rage that year, but which she had not yet seen. While in the rear-view mirror, haloed by the sun, the Badgerline hot-air balloon drifted toward the hill.

Turn. Click. The radio came on with the ignition, permanently set on the Classic Gold station by her older boyfriend. *Nights in white satin, never reaching* – she changed channels. That song was before her time. She wanted something familiar to help her cope and found *Wet Wet Wet* instead, on Radio Wiltshire.

And below the hill, in those caves where gold can lie, those chronicles of old light which lay open between the dragon's claws, turned over another page toward the end.

*   *   *   *   *   *   *

In the year of 1908, that final meeting at the cross-roads was still some little distance away. Grahl's manuscript, carefully and beautifully handwritten, rose in a neat pile on his desk. She saw it one day when she – briefly – visited his room in The Swan Hotel, in Bradford. The papers rose 4" high from the mahogany surface, reflected in the polish like an island in a still lake. Shyly, she flicked through, careful to keep the edges straight, scarcely able to follow what she read, and too embarrassed by the presence of the bed in the same room to have concentrated on the words anyway.

"Seems endless doesn't it?" he said softly, coming up to her from behind and holding her by the waist so that she sighed and wanted to melt back against him. "On and on," he whispered, his whole body against her, lips touching her ear. He smelled of cigarettes and brandy and to Rosie it was gorgeous, the scent of another world. "Sometimes, Rosie, I think it never will end ..."

Then just when she could control herself no more, and turned in order to kiss him, he pulled away as if it had never happened, put on his scarf and hat and opened the door to go. And opened the door as if to say: *Keep away; not yet*; but with an odd air also of: *Can't catch me for a bumble-bee* – as the kiddies chant went.

And so instead of an afternoon of passion between the sheets, in a room above Church Street next to the River Avon, overlooking St Thomas More's church, they 'did' Belcombe Court as you might say now. They met Woodruffe and Blount, the owner and his friend, and toured the estate's stone circle and caves, and circled the conical tumulus known as Bel's Tump which, even today, has never been excavated. But it was a fraught afternoon, the summation of something long arranged but perhaps better cancelled. Grahl smoked a lot but said little, and was clearly slightly drunk. There was some unspoken tension between him and their hosts, plus a sense that this would never be allowed again, and was probably a mistake anyway. And Rosie herself, all churned up by her own juices, was hardly at her best when it came to picking up the images. You didn't need psychic powers to discern that Woodruffe and Blount were less than impressed.

"I'm sorry," said Rosie, shame-faced when the iron gates of Belcombe closed behind them. But Grahl was gracious. It didn't matter. Few things did, he said, as if there were things on his mind – terrible things – which certainly *did* matter, and which put all else in context. Some things she never could see.

"Just do your best tomorrow night, okay? I've got a party arranged. We'll tie it all together."

He left her there in the empty road while he swayed off toward the Barton Steps and back to the hotel, touching the walls of the court at intervals to keep his balance.

Scream said the voice of her frustration, but she never did.

*   *   *   *   *   *   *

Today it is a hospice run by the Dorothy House Foundation, where you can die and have beautiful views. Years before that it was a school for what they then termed 'maladjusted' boys. In Rosie's days it kept changing hands so rapidly from one individual to the next that it never took on the almost human identity that some of the houses in Old Winsley have accrued. As far as she knew then, in 1908, it was owned by a Mr Dancey, a popular writer whose tales of young boys with stout arms, adult hearts and pure ideals were standard reading, it was said, in the dormitories of England. Dancey himself was rarely seen in village life, but whispers passed on through the freemasonry of servants said that he was not quite top-drawer, *pur-sang*. It was rumoured that he loved a woman in Laura Place, Bath, whose husband was adrift in Arctic waters, among the killer whales. It was thought he might have been Jewish, even.

Before Rosie entered the griffin-surmounted gates she could sense an atmosphere within. She could feel it as we might feel the throbbing bass on a modern sound system. Oil and candle torches set on bamboo poles littered the grounds: torches which have now become fashionable again, and sell in large quantities at garden centres on Sundays. The aim was for romance, but the effect was rather tawdry in the half-light of dusk. Someone squeezed at an accordion in one part of the grounds; elsewhere, someone scraped a little more skilfully at a violin, though not together, or with the same tune. Dark was rising from the valley below as the sun came down somewhere near the *Fox and Badger* at Wellow, and people spoke loudly from gin. Stars came faintly in the pale sky, women shrieked in laughter, and spasmodic clapping could be heard. In the gardens, between the shrieks, a man was wearing the hide and head of a bull. He pranced and pounced, leaped and loomed, tickled and goosed with the tail. The bull's head covered his completely; his arms were in the forelegs; the skin was fastened tight at the chest and the rest just flopped loosely below. It was old, very old indeed.

And the women! Well, women who would never have allowed a stranger to touch them so familiarly in normal guise were quite happy, after a gin or two, to allow this unknown bull-man to prod their breasts and buttocks with a dead-beast's tail. It was that sort of mood, or atmosphere, like you can still find today with the Marshfield Mummers or the Padstow 'obby 'oss. The sight of it and very feel of it troubled Rosie greatly. She had glimpsed such things in her visions, in those lost worlds that she had explored with Grahl. But people were different then, when the stones were intact and the circles unbroken, and the bull-men were right for the time and place. Here and now, on the edge of Winsley Hill in the autumn of 1908, with a strange mix of the middle-class, servant class, and the Kellaways around, there was an air about it like a rotting corpse: sickly-sweet; full of infections. To Rosie's inner eye, spirits of the worst kind were drawn to it all like flies to the opened flesh.

The bull-man gave a muffled roar. It might have been her name *Rrrrrose!* which she heard as he lolloped toward her in his obscene parody of ancient things once holy. Rosie drew back. Under the sputtering torches, in the rising dark, the effect of the mask was unnerving. Even the most pathetic specimen of Winsley manhood – and there were many – would have been transformed. The bull-man danced before her from one foot to the other and back again. The tail waved. The whole thing was strangely obscene but compelling also. Yet when the tip of the tail moved slowly but certainly to the point of Rosie's right nipple, that was enough.

"Touch me with that bloody thing," she said, "and I'll rip your head off and shove the horns up your arse."

She didn't have to raise her voice. It didn't need supra-vision of the bull-man to know that she meant it. Besides, Rosie realised, it was only one of the Kellaways in there, acting as Kellaways did when they'd had a drink or three. She could tell, by the tackety boots which the whole family got wholesale from Brown's in Bradford, at a reduced rate owing to family links. The whole hill knew it.

The bull man's tailed drooped and withdrew.

"Dunno what you're so uppity about," said the muffled voice. "My grandad had your gran all ends up in the fields at Danes Bottom, wearing this. Anyone can tell you that."

Rosie blinked in astonishment. Her mouth opened and shut again. The bull-face looked at her impassively, torchlight glinting on the horns. She was about to grab him, perhaps, when a rich brogue from behind said:

"Miss Chant? But you will be looking for Himself, of course." It was Andrews, the Irish butler who had served here through many masters, whose pulled-in stomach gave him an enormous chest and many digestive problems, and whose dishevelled air made him seem exactly what he was: second-rate servant to a third-rate man. "Mr Grahl, I mean. Himself, as we call him."

Did they indeed? thought Rosie, still eager for anything which related to her man.

Himself. She liked that.

"He asked me to be looking for you. He is over there, with some guests, I believe. Can you be seeing that cluster of lights yonder? Yes? Well he is over there."

Rrrrrr! came a half-roar which made her jump as the bull-tail flicked up her nose. She turned with raised fist but the creature disappeared into the shadows, stumbling into them where he couldn't see properly.

The butler laughed. "Ah but you mustn't mind the boy, Miss Chant. It's Mr Grahl's doing, all this …" He waved expansively around, taking in the whole valley and half the hilltop. "He is always after encouraging the country crafts, and the old stories and customs. He is a great man, is Himself, and famous in his own country." The man paused and looked archly at Rosie, head cocked ever-so-slightly to one side, his stomach relaxing a bit so that his chest sagged. "Ah but you'll be knowing such things about him better than myself, I'm thinking!"

She would be. Yes she would. She might have said something, irritated as she was by the mood of the whole place and responding in kind herself, but Charlie appeared then. *Come one Kellaway, come them all,* as they always said. Charlie in the dusk, a tumbler of gin in his hand, pure crystal. See how he'd come along in the world!

"Rosie …" but he swayed, he was well gone. "Rosie …" but his words stuck and hovered, like a small boat mounting a wave.

Rosie turned away. She didn't care if he was upset or not.

"Go and find your mum, Charlie," she told him, snapping the words back over her shoulder as she went, in a way that would stick as painfully in his mind as Grahl's final wave would soon do for Rosie.

She hurried off toward the cluster of lights that hovered below the lumpen black shapes of the yew trees.

*   *   *   *   *   *   *

In our present day, when our senses are deadened entirely, or else addictively sharpened by chemical stimulants, and our morals are strung up on a variety of life-support machines, young lovers can still find outrage and shock amid the perfidies of loving. Rosie-on-the-cusp, just nudging into the 20th century and coming toward the flames beneath the yews like some death's head moth, had none of the anaesthesias we all get now from Hollywood, or the BBC, or the problem pages in the tabloids. There was nothing to prepare her for what she saw. She who had grown up among bull-on-cow, dog-on-bitch, ram-on-ewe, and seen things done between men and women in the corn, was totally unprepared for the sight of Grahl with one hand up Ellie Macleod's skirts, and the other in Beth Macleod's blouse. Plus the pair of them giggling as they always giggled. Well … that was a dagger to the heart. And in the decades to come, with the infinite replays, it was that giggling which upset as much as anything. So banal it was almost evil. None of the passion which she would have expressed. None of the noises of desire and fulfilment. Nothing which echoed the seriousness of the event. Just girlish giggles while Himself rummaged under their clothing and owls flew across the moon.

She turned before he saw her and fled back toward the house, but caught her foot on something and went sprawling onto the cinder path which edged the flowered section of the grounds.

"Buggery! Shite!" she muttered through clenched teeth, where her right hand was ripped by the fall. And she saw Grahl's face above and felt strong arms lifting her to her feet. Yet when she steadied herself it was Charlie's strong arms which had done it, and Grahl just stood there, hands in pockets and hatless, a cigarette in the corner of his mouth and cool as the night sky. As if nothing had really happened.

"You're bleeding," the American said, and he took out a large silk square just as he done at Conkwell, on that first occasion outside the Tea Rooms. "Here," and he brushed the grit off before tying it around and for those brief seconds he was all presence and eye-contact, very deliberate, and Rosie was the only woman in the entire world. Charlie and some others looked on. Charlie was too drunk to be jealous. There were lights and music in the background: the accordion and fiddle came together in an old song about haystacks and wives.

"I've been looking for you!" he charmed. "Mr Dancey's ready. He's got the Luck with him."

And Rosie frowned. Had she imagined it? Had those hands which bound her wounds really been inside the Macleod sisters' clothing?

"Rosie …" he said, and it was so different to the way that Charlie had said it. "Rosie …" and his voice was an adder through the grass: rippling and patterned, full of old knowledge. "Hey lighten up!" he joked, throwing the cigarette to the path and crushing it, and although no-one on the hill had heard such a phrase in 1908, Rosie understood it at once. She lightened up as best she could.

In fact she had no choice: things were coming to an end. Rosie was a spluttering torch that night, but very dim.

*   *   *   *   *   *   *

"Here is the Luck," he said, handing it to her on a cloth and carefully lifting it onto her opened and unwounded left palm.

Grahl spoke softly, reverently, while the drooping and infinitely sad features of Mr Dancey looked on, suffused with the air of someone at the tail end of some grand and destructive passion. There was a scattering of others around the room, behind them, drinks in hand, their best manners firmly fastened in place like their hats on the hat-stand. There were Kellaways and Burts, Grints and Hayes. Almost a symposium of the yeoman classes on Winsley Hill: respectful but not reverential; interested but not committed. And each one with an eye for the main chance as they stood there, balancing goat-like on the rugged lower-to-middling social slopes of their plateau.

The noise outside continued, though more raucously as the alcohol took effect. Someone lit a bonfire, and the sparks shot up into the night and young men kindled it brave. They all said how kind it was of Mr Dancey to throw such a 'do', and how this would never have happened in the old days, and what snobs the rest of them were in their big houses and whatnots. *Rrrrrrraaah!* went the unknown bull-man, as his latest victims giggled in unison.

"Close the windows please!" said Dancey, who saw that the noises from outside were affecting Rosie. Windows were closed, noises muted and Rosie sat there stewing with that delicate silver disk on her palm, tilting it slightly so that the lamp-light glistened off it. She was tempted to close her hand and bend the Luck into a shapeless lump. It was thin, ancient, she could have done it; she was so unsettled it would have been easy, given her mood; and what would have happened to the hill then? She looked at it and looked around, above and beyond the heads. The flames from the large hearth made the great stuffed deer heads on the far wall flicker with a semblance of life. Outside she could still hear the Macleod sisters and the bull-man chasing each other. And inside herself, where all things existed, she felt for the first time in her life somehow dirty as she sat there before them all, palm open, with a single piece of silver on it.

"Rosie Chant, Rosie Chant," said Grahl, caressing her with his voice again. "What do you see?"

What did she see?

She saw the people of the stones and woods and the great bulls slaughtered under the Moon. She saw her mother skinning cats in the shed, by candlelight, and the quick kiss of the man who bought the furs. She saw the Kellaways and Chants in centuries past at loggerheads then as now, in the unstoppable motion of their hate; and millennia before that she saw the small leathery women bringing salt to the tall priestesses by the settlement gates. She saw small things, she saw great things, the essence of the hill; the past and future swirling like water down a plug-hole, the images swept away before she could fix on them. No sooner did she start a scene than it was spun away, hurtling off into some dark continuum where the time-lines conjoined and became one. And the dragon under the hill, whose umbilical this was, stirred slightly in its dreaming.

"People," she said. "They're coming toward the … no, no, there's a single woman – three men – no, the herd is … my mother is … people …"

On and on, start and stop. Like reading torn fragments from the chronicles of old light.

Dancey raised his eyebrows. He too was experiencing something of a vortex: troubled in love and alone, his conscience was swirling in Arctic waters with the husband he put horns on, his mind only just upon the events in his hall. Dancey had read Grahl's first book and envied the man's adventures in writing it. But he couldn't see that there was much in this escapade involving a rough-handed farm girl from the Winsley Lanes.

"Rosie?" said Grahl less soothingly, but Rosie, swirling, was doing her best. She had never known her strange vision go like this before. Maybe it was what she had glimpsed under the yews; maybe it was the power of the Luck, or luck itself. All things thrown together and spiralling. "Rosie, this is important ..."

She knew that. This was going to be the greatest book ever written and she would have it on a shelf in their large house, and their many children would slide past it on their dark and polished floors. Rosie, grabbing toward her own slice of luck, took a deep breath.

"I can see —"

The doorbell rang wildly. Commotion outside. Grahl's face suffused with a brief malevolence that he quickly masked. Andrews the butler whispering into Dancey's ear and Dancey grimacing at the stink of gin on his servant's breath.

"I rather fear that we must bring this, er, fascinating experiment to a premature end. There are two policemen outside who want words with us all generally, but our Miss Chant here in particular."

Rosie blinked rapidly. Her heart beat fast. She put the Luck back on its cushion and felt the vortex slurp away and seal itself.

*   *   *   *   *   *   *

Rosie knelt at Grahl's feet, sobbing. The massively framed portraits of unknown ancestors glowered down at her from the walls of Dancey's study. In her head, the knowledge of her mother found dead in her chair by two policemen on their way to investigate the body found hanging from a tree at Inwoods. Rosie couldn't speak, and yet the images poured through her mind this time: her mother coughing, her pale face and lethargy; the odd things that others had said. Why hadn't she seen? Rosie sobbed, head bent, hands on her knees. She couldn't look at anyone, she couldn't look at all.

"So who, actually, has been murdered?" asked Dancey, unconcerned by the young woman's grief but scenting a story. And before the even younger policeman could answer, Rosie knew – she saw the face and the rope, the stiff tongue, and heard the sound *Wrrrrrrhh!* in her head as if he passed her yet.

80

"Chap from Broughton Gifford, I believe sir," he said, passing his helmet from under one arm to the other, uncomfortable in the presence of fame.

"Reason? Motive?"

"Oh I dunno sir," lied the policeman, who was courting a Kellaway girl and who knew at least one side of everything that happened on the hill. "Domestic upset maybe? Some kind of revenge?" he muttered, keen to protect the dynasty he anticipated.

"And who do you think is responsible?"

Rosie, remembering a perfect night with her mother when the Kellaways had interrupted and she had paid them off with a vision, burst out with: "Mm!" and it might have been the word 'me!' or the first syllable of 'mum!' but the rising sob confused the sound, and she wouldn't repeat it, no matter how many times she was asked. And the policeman didn't press the matter anyway because it was 1908, and justice of sorts had been done and everyone knew it, and the animal mutilations stopped from that night, and Truth in any case was no more than a thin old shape that anyone could bend if they wanted.

That was the way luck went on Winsley Hill. Everyone knew that.

CHAPTER SEVEN

If the chronicles of old light on Winsley Hill (infinitely more enduring than Dancey's tales of pre-pubescent daring) were to fall open naturally in any place, it would be the night when Maggie Chant died and her daughter became a 'murderess'. Folk said for years that was the best party, the best night, any of them had known: all those lanterns and lust, that free drink and scandal and that bull-man ... no-one ever did know for certain who that had been.

On that night too, Andrews had let slip how Rosie had – *ssssh ssssh!* – more or less confessed to murdering the Wheeler. Well, good as. And the Kellaways had kept silent and crossed their fingers, and sent good thoughts toward Rosie that she might not speak in more detail. Who cared about the Wheeler anyway? He was from Broughton Gifford!

So the rumours started across the hill like worms in a sewage plant, gorging themselves on reject matter, growing huge and bizarre. So when Rosie passed anyone in the months after it was always: "Here's Rosie Chant, *ssssh!*" in much the same way as the Wheelers had once gone *Wrrrrrh!* Oh it was so nice to have a scapegoat again.

"That's what she is, a scapegoat!" said Eleanor 80 years later when some things hadn't changed much at all, and phrases such as *there's that Rosie, ssh! She's not deaf!* vied with *that Rosie Chant ... it's all her fault!* as the sayings of the moment, in the Home.

"I don't entirely disagree," said the Manager in the sour voice and infinite and pained wisdom that Managers affect. "She is getting blamed for things that couldn't possibly be her fault. This thing about her clairvoyance or whatever – well, pure nonsense of course. And I am as aware of her good sides as anyone. But for her sake, not mine, I feel that this is no longer an appropriate placement for her." He was tetchy. For some reason his breasts ached.

"Ssssh!" said Eleanor with ire, no longer worried about her contract, having made her own deals with Heggarty via the Sits Vac page in the *Wiltshire Times*. Rosie, who was now officially not deaf at all, looked out of the window, the edge of her brow against the cold glass. She turned, slowly, looked at them.

"This is where I belong," she said simply. "Here." She pointed downward, but she didn't mean the Home. "I belong here, I'm not moving."

Her face turned back to the glass again. She could read that Manager like a book, everyone knew that. No, she wouldn't be going anywhere. Not now. Not now that Himself was back upon the hill.

* * * * * * *

"Think about it Rose," said the Manager, one hand on her elbow up and down the stairs, showing her around *Tigh Aisling*, the half-way house in Brock Street, Bath. "It's informal here, less of a Home and more of a home, if you understand me. Look in here, this would be your room. Look, you can make toast here. Look at the view!" His voice was shaky, having been lambasted at the door by a Scotsman drowning in his own Waters of Life. 'Bluidy English poofter,' had been the drift of it, yet the tramp had been almost reverential toward Rosie.

The old woman looked. Before her was the garden, the park and the houses stretching away into the greyness, up the encircling hills, toward the south and the unseen sun. For some reason she was remembering a time when her mother had bounced her on her lap and told her fairy stories.

"Far, far away ..." she muttered, and the Manager strained to hear that voice and accent from another aeon and wished he could do more about modulating his own, to give it a softer, more feminine sound. Time was running out for him, after all.

Her mother. She remembered also the day when they had buried Maggie Chant along with the skeleton of the Roman baby they had found while digging at Church Farm. Rain poured into the open grave they shared, onto the two paupers' boxes, the little one on top of the larger, and the vicar hurrying the words before the coffins started floating in the hole. And she recalled how the rain had dripped off the brim of Grahl's hat as he stood with his head inclined, in clothes too summery for that world or that season, and proving visibly what they all had known all along – that he did not belong.

"Amen," said the Reverend Walter Hamilton-Smith uneasily, his own finely-tuned and determinedly Christian senses telling him that something about the situation was – if not actually unholy – at very least awry.

Rosie, drenched, was 'off with the fairies' as they said upon the hill. Her eyes were as silvered as an old lady's as she peered through the veil into the Otherworld where her mother walked off into that land where it was always Summer, a fat baby in her arms and happy again, throwing a smile back to Rosie like the sun.

Wait! she cried in her head.

"Mum," she said with her lips.

Grahl touched her shoulder. His hand slipped in hers and squeezed it. No comfort from him, though.

"That was me in there," he whispered as Old Bert turned the soil into the open grave and the vicar squelched off with none of the condolences he normally dispensed like biscuits. "I mean me, myself Rosie. I was that baby. I know it! Call it an ancestor, a previous life – who cares? I've found myself at last, Rosie. And I've still got the little coffin in my room!"

You can see that coffin today, in the Bradford museum. When it is quiet, you can still sense the grief of the parents who placed the child into it and sank it into the hill. And if you can sense closely, and bring your grief onward for fifteen hundred years or so, you can even feel what Rosie felt that day when she became an empty coffin herself: stone cold, desolate, built for reasons of despair and loss.

She squeezed the hair from her brow, wiped her eyes, and was surprised to see Charlie standing there beyond the grave and toward the gate, under an old brolly, hat in hand and head slightly bowed in respect.

"I'll take you home," said Grahl, as she walked to the gate.

"I'll walk you home, Rosie," offered Charlie, lifting his brolly a foot to accommodate her.

Rosie said nothing to either, but walked on through the gate, her grey skirt trailing in the mud and leaving a trail.

"Come," said Grahl, ushering her one way.

"Come with me," offered Charlie simultaneously, and the rain made a song upon the umbrella, each drop exploding into shrapnel, and somewhere beneath all their minds the great dragon within the hill gave what passed as a smirk on its saurian face.

Rosie, whose soul was an empty coffin just then, looked from one to the other, her mind registering nothing.

"Rose?"

"Rosie?"

Although there were no crows, no portents in the heavens to illuminate the fact, her life hinged upon that moment. Charlie stood there holding up his battered old gamp, clean shaven and dressed in his best, splendid in his own style, never more brave in his whole brave life than he was then. He willed Rosie to join him in that small dry space with all of his power. *I love you* he thought to her, but his love had no influence upon that Power which stalked the lanes, and which had brought them to this point outside the church gate, on the edge of consecrated ground, at the mercy of the wind and rain. Grahl, who seemed beyond the touch of any known deity of that era, waited at the other side, wet and sleek, face like a cruel angel, comfortable in his power and control. She looked from one to the other, apparently indifferent to both.

"I'll make my own way," she muttered, uttering a prophecy if only she knew it.

"Well I'll be seeing you," said Grahl pointedly while Charlie, who felt like the Fool in the tarot card who teeters on the brink of the abyss, swallowed his hurt and said nothing.

Rosie lost it then. Nothing is clearer in the chronicles of old light than that – nothing more obvious to the cat-like pupils of the dragon's eye. The three roads where Heggarty stands became a single track with high narrow walls leading to a single place.

*   *   *   *   *   *   *

That night, in a cottage still filled with her mother's things but not her presence, Rosie got what she'd dreamed of for months. Grahl by the fire, steam coming from his wet clothes and tousled hair, limned by the flames behind him. A log popped and sent sparks across the room like meteors. He took off his jacket, his waistcoat, undid his tie and collar and then his cuffs. His eyes transfixed hers. Neither blinked, neither looked away. She matched him. Their movements mirrored. They came toward each other.

As such things go it was not the greatest of seductions. There was sharpness and hurt; there was weight and grinding. It was the coupling of beasts. Charlie could have done it better, given a chance. Grahl bit, Rosie scratched. He squeezed or poked, she tore and thrashed. Pain and blood, bruises down below, grunts and groans. It had the violence of rape but there was full consent. No theft was involved. She took as much as he, and with as much hunger. It was a dark mating, though the fire roared and candles guttered. She hated it, yet she claimed him again and again.

That was the way things went on Winsley Hill, in 1908. What else did she expect?

And later, the calm within and without. Moon and stars and a clear night. Silence descending like a great sigh. Outside, after all the heavy rains, the pond had flooded, filled the whole field with a silver sheet, lapping to the red-painted step of the cottage, bringing the moon's single beam to her feet as she stood there naked, unaware of the cold and indifferent to any human gaze.

"Water," said Grahl softly, his own naked body behind hers, his hands lightly on her hips. "It's a symbol of the unconscious – and what lies below it." Rosie said nothing, thought nothing, felt nothing.

"This flooding ... you've released energies within the land, Rosie Chant. Who knows where this will lead. You are indeed a witch!" he whispered. A shooting star flared into the atmosphere, snuffing itself out eternities above them.

"An old, old lady in le Foret de Paimpont, in Brittany, once told me – and she swore me to secrecy on this, Rosie – that shooting stars are souls coming to earth. Did you know that one?"

Rosie nodded. Everyone knew that. She said nothing. Grahl reached over her shoulder, pointing. "See over there ... Low down. Way down to the horizon? That's Taurus the Bull." He traced its shape with an index finger like a wand. "And that cluster of stars on its back? Yeah? That's the Pleiades. They rise in May and sink in November. Whole nations used them to organise their lives. That's where I come from, I think. Somehow."

Rose kept silent; she couldn't make them out anyway. Something flew across the Moon and spirits flickered at the edges of her perceptions – strands, drifts of coloured consciousness which made veils among the heavens like the Northern Lights.

Childhood's finished she thought, and felt him come hard against her again. *I'm a woman now.*

Dogs barked briefly into the darkness from Potticks Farm, but it should have been wolves. The worst was yet to come.

* * * * * * *

"The best of your life is yet to come," said the Manager as they stood in the empty room looking out, yet neither seeing the same thing. He was talking to the Woman within himself as much as to Rosie, and sometimes one seemed as distant as the other. "The name of this house means House of Dreams. 'Tigh Aisling'. I can get you new carpets, furniture, a remote-controlled telly with subtitles. Your own commode, of course ... just tell me. I just know you'll get on with the other residents. I think Dr McHaffee said you might know one of them from the hospital?"

Rosie fiddled with the plastic poppy that the drunk had given her – on bended knee – at the doorstep. The last time she had had flowers she had found them on a wall, given to her by Powers. Doors closed and opened around the house; she had a sense of people hiding from her and scurrying away like mice. It was cold outside. She knew it was going to snow here soon.

But her true thoughts were 82 light years away upon that flooded field and its silence, remembering how – as if at Grahl's behest – two great swans glided from the night, huge pale shapes surging from the darkness like pteranodons, ancient and awesome, their wings catching the moonlight at angles as they banked and swished onto the surface of the water.

"They mate for life, you know," said Grahl, as they glided over the pond toward them, curious, and then away. And Rosie felt that the spirits of the Lord and Lady who lived within Jug's Grave had taken on flesh for a while to come and see her at this important hour.

They mate for life, you know, echoed the words in her mind then and a million times in the decades which followed. It was the nearest thing to a proposal, or statement of intent, that she was ever going to get from him. She rolled these words over and over in her mind until they became crystalline with pressure: she looked into the crystal and saw, as young lovers will, everything she wanted – and none of it true. Like most seers, she never could see clearly for herself.

"I must show you that coffin soon, Rosie. Real soon. See what you can pick up from that!"

You must, she thought dully. *So you must.*

A gasp of wings, the splashing of water. The swans rose to the stars and were lost.

"Take me out of here," she told the Manager in his House of Dreams. "Now!"

* * * * * * *

"Oh you must see this Rosie!" cried Eleanor excitedly, brandishing the *Wiltshire Times*. "What do you make of that!" The young woman fluttered the broad pages before the old, jabbing her finger at a single item in the Letters Page. Even Rosie, who had seen many wild extremes of behaviour during her lifetimes among the mentally unstable, was impressed by her fervour.

"Read it to me," she said, with an accompanying gesture in the sign language which would not fully leave her.

"Right," replied Eleanor, mastering herself and pushing her dog into the corner with the side of her ankle. "It says: *I am researching my family history. If anyone has any knowledge of the Chant, Dancey, or Vesey-Jones families who lived in the Winsley/Bradford area in the early part of this century, would they please write to Box No 187.* Rosie … the name *Chant*! This could put you in touch with some long-lost relative! You might be somebody's aunt!" cried Eleanor, who still clung to the revised nativity of Rosie Chant.

The old lady looked toward the words but made no attempt to read them. *That's me in there* she thought, sitting back in her chair and lacing her bent fingers together, quietly satisfied though not surprised. She had never doubted that her perceptions were right: that Himself was on the way; that The Man was returning, somehow, after all these years.

And later, after Eleanor had changed the sheets, hoovered the room and dusted generally, while mentally composing a letter on Rosie's behalf, the youngster said: "Oh … and where were you yesterday? I heard that the boss took you for a jaunt to the market in Bradford. Have a nice time?"

Rosie smiled. She looked at her laced fingers. At her age, with that degree of twist, it was difficult to make them into the comfortable cup of her youth. It hurt a little, but reminded her of where she was, and stopped her getting lost within the loop of dreams and remembrance. Physical pain, which lives for the present and is said to carry no memory, could do that for her. "I was … at some place in Bath. A large house. They called it the House of Dreams, but it weren't that."

Eleanor was thunderstruck. "Tigh Aisling? That bloody place? I was promised – I mean *promised* – that nothing would be done without my involvement. *Nothing!* Listen … you weren't pressured into anything were you? No? Well … good. But don't make any choices now Rosie. Don't make any choices, okay?"

Rosie Chant nodded and closed her eyes, and snuggled into her chair for a nap. No choices were necessary. She was Heggarty: some things were inevitable. Heggarty made the three roads come to her.

"Thank you," she whispered, touching Eleanor's head in a kind of benediction as the young woman bent and tucked a colourful crochet blanket around her legs.

Eleanor rocked back. For a moment she felt as if a gentle light had surged in her mind's eye – though only for the duration of the touch.

"Oh, my, you'll have a baby," said Rosie tenderly, almost whispering, stroking Eleanor's cheek with the back of her sickle-shaped hand. "It'll have blonde hair, green eyes, and —"

"Rosie please!" said the younger woman sharply, who was afraid of the road into the future and what might lie by the side. Anyway, she had not had sex for months and saw little chance of it in the years ahead. What man these days really wants to Communicate, eh?

Rosie smiled and nodded, only too familiar with this kind of fear. "I'll er, well … I'll … I'll leave you be Rosie. Have a nice nap."

Eleanor rose, slapped her thigh and called her dog. "I'll get that letter off to the *Wiltshire Times* right away. Anything you want to say? No? Well I'll see you later." The back of her knees were weak as she left the room. Nerve endings prickled on her back.

God how she wanted to believe in the old lady's vision!

* * * * * * *

"I'll leave you be then" was more or less what Grahl had said when he left her that morning at cock-crow, which was late and indiscreet by the standards of the farm workers. The Lanes, the fields, were already thronged, and it was like a bayonet to Charlie Kellaway's heart when he saw the American leave the cottage and skirt around the flooding to scramble over the nearest wall.

"Good morning gentlemen – and ladies!" he said, cheerily enough and cool as you like as he strode into the rising light toward his rooms at Bradford.

"We know what *he* 'ad then," said one of Charlie's brothers in a mixture of scorn, envy and embarrassment. Charlie went cold, but managed a weak smile. He felt sick, and wanted the earth to swallow him up. He wanted that last more than anything else, but he had to wait a few years before the German artillery tried to oblige him in a literal sense.

"She was never worth it Charlie," whispered his young aunt later when she managed to single him out. She knew the truth, and something about passion too. Charlie nodded vehemently. "Besides, a lot of folk reckon she murdered her own mother you know, as well as that Wheeler who tried to touch her up."

He nodded again. It was nonsense of course, they both knew the real truth. But real truth has qualities of a doctor's knife and it was bandaging he needed then, not surgery.

"Bleedin' Chants … always did think themselves above the rest of us."

Charlie, who had not come from anywhere near as grand as Grahl's Pleiadic cluster, said nothing. Charlie had plummeted to earth after his brief soar amid the clouds above the hill. By the bare walls near Conkwell, he sat down and wept.

* * * * * * *

Eleanor Brittle waited in a window-seat in the Scribbling Horse café in Bradford, next to where Market Street, Silver Street and Masons Lane run into each other, joined in a tau-cross by a mini-roundabout. Great lorries squeezed through the narrow streets; tyre edges bulged ominously as they clipped onto the pavements to avoid oncoming traffic; gears and air-brakes echoed in the narrow canyons of that tau like bull elephants. Her heart was beating strongly, she couldn't say why. She had a sense of immanence, although she couldn't have used that term. It was like being a child again, on Xmas Eve, was her nearest comparison. She had only spoken to the man on the phone the night before, and little enough had been said then, yet she couldn't sleep afterward. His voice had been honey; she felt as if she'd been stroked. When you're nearly thirty as Eleanor was, undeniably attractive yet inexplicably alone, voices on phones arranging dates can have that effect.

She knew him at once of course: that indefinable quality of dress and attitude which singles out young Americans abroad – yet with that same added reek of Old Money clinging to his expensive clothes like Grahl's cigarette smoke.

Before he had even got across the road to her side she had assessed him and saw that he was good: angular features and odd lines … other women might have thought him a bit of a dork. But Eleanor, who bought books on the Holy Grail and Lost Treasures of Britain, fancied, even as they made first eye-contact over the condiments, that she saw strange and holy depths within him.

"Hi," he said, offering his hand, and love had already started to rise in her soul, like flames.

Oh please God, don't let me screw this up! Not this time! she implored to much the same unseen Power which had influenced Rosie's life too, and had brought her into the presence of this luminous young man.

"Hello," she replied, shyly, but only glad that she'd gone on that course for developing and expressing interpersonal skills.

* * * * * * *

It was an afternoon of wonders, revelations ... and he wouldn't let her pay for anything. They couldn't believe it, they kept saying, that Eleanor's Rosie and the Rose in those old, hand-written journals were the same one. It was astounding, and she could hardly take her eyes off him.

But look ... and look ... he kept saying, pointing to some new correlation in the manuscript and touching her lightly on her hand each time. And, all right, he had a tendency to slurp his coffee, but what did the English know about coffee anyway? And he spoke rather loudly in that small and crowded place, but that was just his way – such openness was so refreshing. Plus he wasn't a vegetarian, but she found herself respecting his viewpoint so beautifully expressed: "Western man needs meat, Miss Brittle," he had said, and she bowed her head and blushed; she just loved his candour.

Eleanor whirled, frizzes in her hair and Hecate at her back, soaring toward love and the grand passion. She couldn't have seen that the great dragon Time had folded its wings and was about to swallow its own tail once more. She couldn't have read that chapter in the chronicle of old light which started: *Spring came again, and nothing changes much on Winsley Hill.*

* * * * * * *

"I still can't believe it," she said, not exactly truthfully, but more because her interpersonal skills weren't up to the pitch of her emotions. She was perched on the edge of his bed in the Swan Hotel, pages in her lap, various old books at either side on the blue quilt. Light slanted in the window, made the cornflower wallpaper glisten. Eleanor, who had studied crystal healing as well as other alternative therapies, felt that she swam in a warm, pure ocean.

"When Rosie said she was from No Man's Land we thought she was being cryptic as usual. She would never say more than she had to."

He showed her the Ordnance Survey map he had bought in the Ex Libris Bookshop, in The Shambles.

"No, I checked it out with Mr Jones at the bookstore. You have to be local to know this place. There's no signposts, apparently, nothing to see."

It was true. In Winsley today, plugged into their internets and reflecting from space with their satellite dishes, few have ever heard of Rosie's Wood, or Rosie's Pond, or No Man's Land – or have any glimmering that a stone circle exists (as fragmented as their lives) less than a mile away as the crow flies.

"And she really is – what? – 100? This ..." and she indicated the sprawl of writing and the little books, "this is really my Rosie? Your great grandmother?"

Edward Grahl II nodded, a face somewhere between that of Puck and the Archangel Raphael. He was on his haunches in front of her, balancing, face wondrous and level with hers.

"It seems so. These here are the old guy's diaries. Here, look, details of meetings, payments and 'other things' in a kind of code that I haven't yet been able to crack."

"Was there anything between them?"

"Did they get it on, you mean?"

Eleanor gave a weak laugh and could have killed herself, but nodded anyway.

"Yes they did. He got her pregnant, and the little boy she had was my grandfather."

Eleanor Brittle, who up until then had lived a life so flat you could see her gravestone at the end of it, had often yearned for something scandalous to look back upon. She was deeply moved by all this.

"So what happened?" she asked.

"Well, extrapolating from the documents I found, plus whispered family lore, it seems that he just upped and left her."

"Bastard!" she said, with real feeling, and then quickly apologised, spilling the papers onto the floor and apologising again.

"Ah heck, don't say that," he grinned as they both scrabbled on their hands and knees to pick up the sheets and put them back into their original order. "My great grandfather, after whom I was named, was widely held to have sold his soul to the devil. Only the devil being in this case the woman he was married to before he came here. The 'rich bitch from Georgia' they all called her. The things they said about her ... but it seems from his final diary entry, here look: 'Summoned back with dire threats. I cannot afford divorce.'"

They were sitting on the floor, leaning back against the bed.

"Look at the date!" said Eleanor, pointing, a whole side of her body lightly against his.

"November 10th, 1908. My god, 82 years ago today *exactly*! How do you like that for synchronicity?"

Oh she liked it fine. And she liked the smell of his aftershave, and she liked those inevitable motions and pressures of his arm against hers which would lead into those acts of seduction which, like stitching, bind together the chronicles of old light down the ages.

"Yep, he was a bastard okay, though I never met him. Died the day I was born, in fact, which always left a great mark on my family and me too, if truth were told. Genetically of course the real bastard was Rosie's child, my grandfather. There are not a whole lot of us Grahls left, but we're all of us descended from him, as Edward Grahl's wife Helen Gwen was apparently infertile."

They were leaning against each other quite firmly now. Rhythms of apparently accidental and unconscious touch were coming into play.

"How did he get to America then?" she asked, and when he took her hand and shrugged, and opened up her palm as if to read her life-line, as if they were the oldest and most familiar friends on the planet, she knew something of what Rosie had felt amid the criss-crossing Lanes so long before, and came close to her at the last.

"I don't rightly know. I can find no more diaries. This manuscript was severely – no, savagely – edited to form this little book here *The Oldest Faith in Celtic Lands*. I think it was Helen Gwen who had a hand in that. My relatives would say nothing more. I don't think they knew, to be honest. Maybe Rosie sold the baby. People did then. Hell, they still do!"

Eleanor was breathing hard, though she controlled herself.

"No," she said firmly. "It would have been taken away. I know it, somehow. That's why she was put in the asylum. I phoned Dr McHaffee from Devizes and he told me that old mental hospitals had, until recently, hundreds of old ladies up and down the country who had simply had children out of wedlock and were put away because their own emotions couldn't cope with the stigma and the scorn. After a while, he said, surrounded by true schizoid and psychotic patients, they themselves started acting as society meant for them to act. They just lost touch with normality, and were wracked with guilt, loss, fear – well, you name it. Then when two World Wars gave everyone better things to do than root out the injustices done to the likes of Rosie, they just got even more forgotten. It was McHaffee's own personal crusade, he told me, to look after women like this. Mind you, there's been so much trouble at his place in Bath, 'Tigh Aisling', that I wouldn't want my Rosie to go there …"

She prattled, she knew that. The words came unevenly. He was holding her palm open, stroking his hand over hers, from wrist to tip. Every line, loop, whorl, mount and intimation of destiny was stroked out clear as a map for those who knew the symbols, and could place the signposts.

"I don't know," he said, fascinated by this sudden power he seemed to have over this lovely young woman. In his own country he had only ever had one girl and she had been after his Porsche more than his personality – which his fellows at school had assessed as negligible. He could be happy here, he thought, below the grey skies, among the narrow streets and narrower paths, if they all acted as Eleanor did. It was his *difference*, he knew that; which found expression in his accent, which he used again now, keeping eye-contact, watching her reactions to his words, feeling her move against him. She was putting out, he knew it. She was trying to hit on him. "Well, certainly such dynasty of Grahl's as exists today is entirely derived from this Rose Chant, who gave my great grandfather such a weird few months in 1908. It's funny … I feel like I came home. I can't wait to meet her."

But he would wait, for Eleanor Brittle sat on the floor, on the light-blue mandala patterns of the dark blue carpet, drowning below the light which shafted through the window, seeing nothing outside but sky. They both stopped talking. There was traffic noise outside like the moan of the sea. They looked at each other, and Eleanor realised that you didn't have to talk to Communicate. She heard seagulls outside like white crows, omens of a storm at sea. She felt that her whole destiny hinged upon the next few seconds.

"Oh … would you kiss me?" she pleaded, pushing the papers aside and putting her lips to his.

If only it had been so easy for Rosie Chant, she might have gained her freedom from the hill and changed a world.

* * * * * * *

That first night Rosie Chant spent having sex with Edward Grahl was also the last, yet it was not the last sex she ever had upon the hill. In the years after she left, when her memory was still green, and for some months before, it was rumoured that she was anyone's and everyone's.

94

"Come one, come all!" they sniggered, and even Charlie said it, though he didn't rightly mean it that way. She became in the minds of some, especially the Reverend Walter Hamilton-Smith, like Wiltshire's answer to the Whore of Babylon, although the cognoscenti from the Old Tea Rooms recalled Grahl's talk about the *sheila-na-gigs*, those stone ladies with the exposed genitalia who adorned many a church wall in olden times.

And the essence of the rumours were all perfectly true, yet sometimes the chronicles of old light can be so blinding that we miss the footnotes, the addenda, or those scribbled comments in the margins that are added for future reference lest we forget. Rosie Chant's footnote might have read: *There was more to it than that: I had no choice.*

Rosie, who had never read the Book of Genesis but knew all about paradise, serpents, trees and temptations, understood The Fall better than anyone. When she made that fateful walk from her cottage to the barn near Inwoods, when the moon was full and red on the last night of October, when the Two Worlds are traditionally at their closest – when she made that walk she was already plummeting …

* * * * * * *

It may have been Hecate's owls which called to her, drew her: those crows which seemed everywhere and ominous by day, she neither saw nor heard at night. She mentioned this to Grahl once and he had said, musingly: "I often wonder if crows are not avatars of daylight's shadow." He said that often afterward, before learned company, and they all gave learned nods or made articulate objections, but she hadn't understood it at all. She never understood much of what he said, actually. And if only, like Eleanor-in-lust, she had begged him to kiss her in those first few days the whole affair might have come to a head and fizzled out before any harm was done, as modern affairs so often do.

In the years to come she would never know what brought her from her bed and made her cross the fields to Inwood, pacing one of the ancient, curving, ceremonial paths that she had glimpsed so often in vision with Grahl. Perhaps it was the owls which woke her, and the lights from the woods which intrigued her conscious mind in a way that our present and hard to satisfy generation would not understand. Or perhaps it was the spirit of the hill whose own secrets had been prised from it in the previous months, which was demanding its own kind of payment.

Certainly she walked as if entranced: essentially aware yet curiously compelled. The bright spirits of the Old Folk whose lives she had spied on were out in force, walking behind her as if in procession. The old stones which had once formed an avenue at this point seemed to have risen from the soil again, glistening in the light of the moon and her magic. The path beneath her bare feet, which should have been the dull, cold mud of autumn, shimmered faintly with the crush of stars. Those of us who have scanned the ever-becoming yet ageless stories in the chronicles of old light on sacred hills throughout the land, might understand that her walk that night was something of a précis to the whole tale – a ritual summary, which tied up some loose ends and energies, and brought the cruel patterns of life into sharp definition. So when she heard the owls and saw the spikes of light spearing out from the distant woods, and made that slow ritual journey in her shift across the fields and between the worlds, Rosie Chant was not herself.

In the years to come her memories of that night were to remain confused. Perhaps it was the effect of the strange cigarettes that Grahl had left with her; but more likely that her senses had blotted the worst details out, in order to cope. It was as if she had had one of those Near Death or Out of the Body Experiences that they talk about now, in which she seemed to look down upon herself, and floated over the whole scene.

That body she saw, shameless in its white shift and oblivious to the cold, was hers. Yet she was not of it. She remembered: the clearing in the woods near Jug's Grave; the bonfire and the ruined, lightning-struck barn; the cocks fighting in a ring of men; that stupid bull-man sitting on a rafter of the barn dangling his tail between his swinging legs. And she remembered the silence which fluttered down into the clearing when they all became aware of her, bringing with it a kind of awe – or was it dread?

Our chronicles, which exist in far more than three dimensions, can tell what happened next in many ways, each level of perception laid upon the last like geologic strata, complete with flaws and upsurges, faults, and magma of its own kind. On one level they were no more than the working elements of the manhood on Winsley Hill, fresh from the *Fox and Hounds* and indulging in some illegal cock-fighting with some pitch-and-toss on the side. They still wore their working clothes, or uniforms: the young constable and drayman; the milkman and knife-sharpener; a private from the Wiltshire Yeomanry and the miller's son; the butcher, baker and candlestick maker. But sometimes, even in the drabbest life of today, we can take on atmospheres and patterns; we can link with energies, events, or consciousnesses that are other or greater than ourselves. Thus on another level Rosie in her shift was a priestess in her grove that night, giving to the tribe what priestesses such as her always gave, while the spirits of the past encircled them and looked on.

"She were askin' for it," they said afterward.

"Nipples like organ stops."

"Come one, come all – her mother was just the same!"

And she didn't resist when they carried her into the shell of the barn and had her, one by one. It wasn't her, somehow, for she was above them all, as Chants had always felt themselves to be.

No it wasn't at all clear, that night. She was numbed, though not from the cold. And the joke of it was the ceaseless thrusting of this gang bang hurt her a lot less than her night of love and passion with Grahl. And as man after man covered her, again and again, she was aware of the bull-man above, his horns glinting from the shadows, and she could have sworn that she saw Grahl there too, standing just behind, watching it all impassively.

"Bit of luck there," muttered one, buttoning himself up and walking away, talking as lightly as if he had just caught a fish.

"Don't get much of that on *this* hill!"

* * * * * * *

Next day, the crows. In little clusters, scattered around the cottage like ragged priests. Great white clouds scudding in a pale sky. She felt drunk, though she hadn't been drinking. If she had been born 70 years later she might have felt rather drugged. And although she had no idea how she had got back to bed again, she knew it had not been a dream. Besides, too many men on the hill around were feeling much the same way, and acknowledging the fact that it really did happen.

She took a lot of virginities that night and – in their eyes at least – turned boys into men and made their lives begin.

Skraaaah! Skraaaah!

Rosie, lying unclean in her ragged bed in the crumbling house, on the small and obscure plateau, felt more alone than any woman there had ever felt.

She saw Grahl a few days after that. Desperate to talk she scribbled a note with a stub of pencil, in her best and scarcely-used writing, begging to meet him. It was addressed to him c/o the Swan Hotel. She posted it at 6 am and get a reply by the third delivery at 2 pm. Such things were possible in 1908, and not wondered at.

She met him by the gate where he had taken that first kiss, after the humiliation down Murhill. It was his idea. The gate was padlocked. The ground was a mass of muddy tracks. A knackered old black mare, its back sagging in line with its belly, snorted mist from its nostrils and looked balefully at her. She was wearing her best, though it was out of season: long red dress, white belt, neat white shoes that were wholly inappropriate to the mud. At that place, at that time, she looked and felt rather pathetic as she leaned against that post which had once been a standing stone, afraid to meet the eye of anyone who came past in case everyone was talking about her. Which they were. Even today, there can be few secrets on that plateau: mainly denials, or misplacements of guilt. The whole hill knew by 9 am that Rosie Chant had sent Edward Grahl a letter; and with the psychometry of malice, they all had some idea as to its contents. As she stood with her back to the cold grey stone, she felt she could hear them muttering, like wind through dry leaves.

Grahl arrived at last by carriage. Perhaps she picked up vibrations in the road, or read the distant body language of animal and the two humans it pulled, or else perhaps she saw things with her inner eye … whatever the explanation, she knew, as they clopped nearer, that it was essentially finished. The white star on the black face of the horse nodded up and down. Rosie felt dread: she felt winter's approach and the hard earth to come. It was as if that horse which pulled Grahl along the Lanes was privy to the secrets of the Power which ruled them, and managed to hint at the future in its long and doleful countenance.

Her man dismounted and briskly told the driver to go on ahead a little way and wait. He wouldn't be long. That was answer enough for Rosie. It hijacked all that she wanted to say. He pulled his heavy coat around himself and pulled the belt taut, and he stood there unassailable.

"You wanted me," he said, and it wasn't even a question. Years and years later when she replayed it in her head it could have been said as "*You* wanted *me*!", which could be interpreted as: "So it's not *my* fault!" Or else the emphases would change and it became: "You *wanted* me", which might mean it was her fault again for lusting after him. But in truth that day there was no emphasis, no inflexion, just three simple words like blank slates on which every possibility of love and treachery could be recorded.

"I … er … I …" she made a cup with her hands, and her fingers gave her no pain at all at this end of her time, but what she saw within the chalice hurt her deeply.

"If it's about the work, I've still got some loose ends. I'd like another attempt at that Luck, and I'd surely like you to see that stone coffin. In fact I'm pretty much straight with my notional family tree these days – but now look, I'll tell you about it next time, okay?"

Rosie stood there in the mud in her best dress and shoes, unlaced her fingers and flung up her hands in a submission of despair, shaking her head and closing her eyes so that she wouldn't have to meet his. There were crows in her head and snakes writhing and hissing in her heart; the air felt wild, crackling, although it was entirely still. If only she could have said "Oh … would you help me?" with the same ease that Eleanor Brittle would ask to be kissed, then something might have given way within him. But she was a woman, and it was 1908, and he was from another world: Rosie Chant, who pulled root crops from the ground and had a labourer's hands, knew her place within that world and upon its levels.

"I'll see you then," she said softly, turning her back to hide the tears and walking off back home, hoping against hope that he would come running after her, though he never did.

Men! cried the spirit of Rosie's mum who watched it all from another level of despair, echoing the cry of all women from everywhere.

Skraaaaah cried the crows, those incarnations of Rosie's own shadows, saying much the same.

*   *   *   *   *   *   *

When you learn to scan the chronicles of old light you need not do so more than thrice: once to see life as chance; twice to see it as coincidence; but the third time to see it all as the curve of an inevitable pattern. Through time and human wisdom the ancient happenings seem to summarise themselves, withering into spirals that are so like the double-helix within: twists and turns that we can learn to anticipate; repetitions like genes that we can isolate and study.

When Grahl left her for that final time in No Man's Land, driving off into the West, it was her birthday. It was also St Catherine's Day which was a big event in Bradford in 1908, with its street fayres and catten cakes and a muted kind of riotry. That same Catherine who has now become a circular firework pinned on gateposts, fizzing around with bewildering speed and threats of sparks – not unlike Rosie-in-a-whirl when Grahl scorched her. That same Catherine whose symbol of an equi-armed cross within a circle was, as Grahl pointed out, not dissimilar to that inscribed upon the Luck. St Catherine, he argued, was merely the Christianisation of that primordial Goddess who once ruled the tribes upon the hill.

Grahl had argued lots of things which had seemed world-changing at the time but which didn't matter at all now. Not when she was 18 and desperately alone, hated upon the hill and pregnant.

Yet Rosie survived. She survived on her savings at first that were left over from the handsome wage that Grahl had paid. And then she received a bundle of notes which – heart-leap – she thought had come from Grahl, but were really from Mr Harkes who had been so moved by her powers that day in the Old Tea Rooms. Once, twice, but never thrice, the Reverend Walter Hamilton-Smith brought offerings with mutterings, but the people of the hill kept away. After all she was a double-murderess; and the menfolk seemed to have other knowledge of her sins, too, that it was unwise to pry into.

The child was Grahl's, she knew that. No, she *knew* it, she thought, playing with the emphases again and again as if to affect the pattern. But no-one else knew it. The bastard when it came could have been an expression of the working classes upon the hill, an incarnation of every man's darkness and desire. A crow-child if ever there was one. By the early months of 1909 she could feel it flapping within and watched her belly grow, with horror. As they would say today, with no knowledge of the betrayal, rape, and metaphors involved, she started to go downhill.

So Rosie Chant went mad according to the accepted nostrums of the day, and that suited them fine. There were things they could do about madness. And when she (alone and ignorant) gave birth to the crow-child during a night of cold and driving rain, it was as if the Power within the Lanes intervened directly and sent the cat-man from Trowbridge to the back door, unknowing of her mother's death, in search of skins but cutting the baby's cord instead before placing it in a blanket and going on for help. Which was when she saw the baby for the first and only time: shock of black hair, ancient unfocused eyes looking right through hers – a bloodied crow-baby in a cat-man's arms.

"Take it away!" she cried. "Take it away!"

And they took it away. There was no chance to get to love it. That was Harkes' doing too. He had taken it upon himself to write to Grahl of Rosie's condition. Discreet correspondence had followed plus some less discreet telegrams. Monies were paid and people were made ready for whenever it happened, and so one small scandal made its way to another world beyond the West, while Rosie found herself being hurled toward Tartarus at last, and the narrow walled corridors of the asylum in Devizes.

In the chronicles of old light on different levels of different hills, in different ways, it happens all the time. Indeed, not long after she gave birth one of the Macleod sisters did so too, though the Macleod wealth kept a far tighter control of the gossip. Even so, when they were sent away from Wiltshire entirely it got about that Grahl was the father of this one – although another stream of rumour insisted that Black John himself was responsible – but Rosie never heard any of that.

She wouldn't have cared, in her state. When the two men came with their secure cart and took her away screaming, and people watched with varying degrees of joy, discretion, or guilt, they prised her from the hill like the Luck from its earthen grave. The Luck would end up in the museum in Devizes, where it can still be seen today: Rosie would become a museum-piece in that same town's asylum, long forgotten.

Though if truth were told she never left the hill at all.

CHAPTER EIGHT

The mood in the Home was intense; everyone bar Rosie was on edge. People seemed to be snapping at each other all the time for no clear reason, and there was a marked increase in night-soiling. Both staff and residents complained that money had gone missing from purses, wallets, and bedside cabinets. Everyone blamed everyone. The number of maintenance requests on the flimsy green pro-formas almost quadrupled: windows wouldn't close or else refused to open; doors would stick in their jambs; floors didn't seem, well, quite as level as before, and the water in the baths was noticeably deeper at the tap ends.

"It's falling apart," muttered one of the colonels (retd.) to the Manager, wielding his zimmer frame like a riot shield and jabbing it in the air around him in his rage at unseen things and cross-dressing perverts. "Wish I'd stayed at Arnhem!" he'd cry. Others, agreeing, thought that the Home was now also haunted, for they had seen strange lights within the corridors and in the grounds outside, and seemed to hear disembodied whispers in the most unlikely places. Their nape hairs prickled. They felt bewildering sweeps of cold in the pits of their stomachs which had nothing to do with room temperatures, or the freak snow which had all but cut off nearby Bath.

She'll have to go thought the Manager grimly, stalking the carpeted corridors as implacably as the Power which stalked the Winsley Lanes, his anticipatory silk stockings sighing under the still-obligatory male trouser legs. He was quite certain that the epicentre of all these seismic and psychological disturbances was to be found within the calm figure of Rosie Chant. The previous day she had been observed in the grounds in her night dress at noon, signing furiously toward the distant hill. Now the Manager's *rational* mind opined that the old lady was doing no more than talking to herself in sign language, telling herself an excruciatingly banal tale of life and old age. But there was his feminine and intuitive side which saw it in another light, an older light, and which made Rosie look like the priestess of some forgotten cult, summoning deities from a thunderous sky.

Rosie however was oblivious to all this. She wore her best grey dress and black shoes, plus a nice long hooded blue overcoat that she had stolen from one of the night staff, and pinned a plastic Armistice Day poppy on her left breast in remembrance of her own Great War between the light and darkness within. Her pockets bulged with money; sandwiches and cakes were crammed into her handbag; she was using a warm iron to flatten a silver milk-bottle top on the marbled surface of the brew-up area next to her room.

The Manager strode up, all clip-board and purpose, ignoring the pleas of the other residents who wanted a word.

"Rosie, I can't fudge the issue any longer. I'm afraid you must leave us, and I strongly recommend you accept the place that has been offered you in Tigh Aisling."

She carried on ironing the little disk, then held it to the light from the window and saw that it was good. The pattern that she had pressed into it with the flat tip of a small screwdriver had held, despite the ironing, and was even more like the original on the Luck as she had remembered it. The equi-armed cross within the circle: the little criss-crossings like those of life and its patterns …

"Everything and everyone to its rightful place," she said, turning to the Manager with a seraphic smile.

Was that a yes? It was a yes!

"Rosie I —"

"You'd better come quickly!" cried an ashen-faced secretary, spinning around the corridor and almost colliding with her boss. "You've got a big crack!" she cried, without any sense of irony. "Your wall's got a crack in it so wide you can see outside. And I think it's getting bigger."

That was the last time the Manager saw Rosie: standing before an open window, sun at her back, the silver disk held up like a Communion wafer and a look of bliss and benediction on the old woman's face. They disappeared around the corner and up a short flight of stairs toward their own kind of oblivion. Rosie waved to the empty space, slid the new Luck carefully into the little pocket on her left breast, beneath the plastic poppy, and went off to meet the taxi that she had ordered. She could no longer carry the Home as she had done for these past few years. She had a Man to meet after all, and a life of her own to live at the last.

* * * * * * *

Eleanor was busy soaring through her own kind of heaven and streaming light behind her like a shooting star, unable to believe her own luck. She had seen little enough of that in recent years. An afternoon of sex followed by an evening of passion which flowed into a night of sustained desire which woke into a morning of wonder – and love. When they decided that they really should get dressed now to meet his great grandmother for the first time, it was already 11am on the 11th day of the 11th month. The small military band which had thumped out a tune across the river at the war memorial went silent. The contingent of soldiers stood in perfect ranks. A scattering of old men and women stood with heads bowed, trying to Remember.

"Can I drive?" she asked him at the car, oblivious to such things in the world around. He'd hired a large saloon with power-steering and mobile phone and electrically operated windows. "With these narrow streets and steep hills," she said, trying to come back to earth again, "power-steering makes life so much easier." She spun the wheel with one finger and mirrored his own smile, shyly. The car surged up Market Street then turned off into Newtown, heading toward the hamlet of Turleigh.

"I'll take you the pretty way," she said, full of herself.

"Sure won't be as pretty as you, Eleanor."

Eleanor, who was directing her own destiny with power at her command, could have died just then with bliss and benediction also.

"Soon be at the Home," she said blushing, scorching into this new atmosphere of Grahl's.

* * * * * * *

"No Man's Land?" asked the taxi driver half-turning toward Rosie in the back seat, her looped silver ear rings jangling beneath dyed black hair which conspicuously drew attention to the tides of middle age. "Never heard of it."

"Winsley then," said Rosie with a certain scorn before settling back with her hands on her lap, imperious.

"Winsley then," echoed the younger woman, who had had a hard day of it already and could have done without this fossil. The clock started, the taxi pulled away and crawled down the drive at regulation speed with its old diesel engine rattling and the strong smell of take-away pizza wafting into the nostrils at intervals. Behind them, weakened by rain, fire and wind, a whole front wall of the Home was collapsing in a cloud of dust which rose in the still air like an escaping genie.

The driver neither heard nor saw: she was listening to her Bonnie Tyler tape with *It's a Heartache* playing, and concentrating on getting into the fast-flowing stream of traffic on the main road. *Oh god*, she muttered, for she needed a new clutch and the cab didn't always respond as it should. The driver of a small white minibus filled with children slowed and flashed his lights to let them go. *Thanks*, she muttered again, while Rosie waved one hand like the Queen and smiled at them all.

The taxi strained up Winsley Hill, throwing out smoke. "Off to see your family?" asked the driver, angling the mirror to see her passenger's face. "No? Oh well ..." Some wanted to talk, some didn't. She pressed a button on the cassette and the song slid into *Total Eclipse of the Heart*. Her head nodded slightly from side to side, in rhythm.

"What's your name?" asked Rosie suddenly, jabbing her shoulder and making eye contact through the mirror. The old woman's eyes, in the angled light, were pure silver, almost startling. The driver kept her own eyes on the road and changed down to second to manage the steepest curve.

"Dulcie Galloway."

"Kellaway?"

"Galloway."

A long pause and tightening of the lips. The air in the cab at once seemed cool, acid. The driver felt uneasy. She was getting too old for this lark.

"Is that your married name?"

Dulcie shook her head; she was used to that question by now and it caused her no pain to give the honest answer. "Never married, not me. Nobody'd have me." The ear rings shook like wind-chimes and the air warmed again, became gentler. Dulcie fiddled with the broken knob on the heater. The car had seen better days, like herself.

"Then I knew your grandfather, Charlie Kellaway. It was him wasn't it?" There was no question in Rosie's mind. Her scowl went; a great understanding flowed across the fissures of her face.

"Charlie, yes. But – *Lunatic*! You bloody *lunatic*!" she yelled over her shoulder and then into the rear view mirror, bouncing her fury toward the large car which had sped downhill toward them, drifting over the line and dangerously close to a head-on collision. She caught a micro-second glimpse of the young woman one-handed at the wheel, unconcerned, the man next to her laughing. "Honestly!" she cried to her passenger. "Young people today are so bloody irresponsible. I'm glad I never had kids, really *really* glad!"

On and on. On and on. Rosie smiled.

"Right, where in Winsley then?" asked Dulcie as they approached the old part of the village and the murderous through-road that still awaited its bypass.

Rosie waved her hands in the air, it didn't matter. Then she held up a bundle of notes and told Dulcie she would have all of these, and it suddenly didn't matter to Dulcie either, who kept her fingers crossed that it wouldn't go wrong as it usually did in this job.

So they drove, and both of them were trembling: Dulcie from the near-crash and Rosie from her sense of immanence. They drove through Old Winsley and into that emotional dimension which impinges upon ours and brought Rosie's childhood and youth alive once more in little bursts of almost unbearable remembrance. The old schoolhouse, the old dairy, the old Wheatsheaf … like bookmarks in the chronicles, flipping them open at her past so that she could almost see the pig-tailed little girl that had been herself skipping in the flesh through the narrow street and alleys. Dulcie could never have dreamed that her old and smoking Citroen BX with its ailing clutch, near-bald tyres, troubled gas-suspension and almost-expired tax could have made such a magical transition between the worlds.

The old part of the village was almost deserted as far as Dulcie could see, but to her passenger it was thronged. The two of them made a right pair: Rosie looking for her past and being driven through it by Dulcie, who had idle dreams of a future when she didn't have to scrape a living by doing this – though Lord knows it would only ever happen if she got herself a Man.

"Who're you waving to?" she asked.

"Me," said Rosie cryptically, though it was no more than truth.

She waved to the child she had been and whom she could still see, running through the village like the wind, and laughing.

"The Lanes next," she added when they had come back to the main road. "Do they still exist? Do you know them?"

Dulcie knew them. In the rear-view mirror Rosie waved the wad of money again and promised it would all be hers.

"Wherever you want," she said, crunching into second gear and chugging off.

* * * * * * *

"Oh god!" said Eleanor when they arrived at the Home and saw the devastation. "Oh shit! Oh bloody –"

Grahl touched her arm, squeezed gently. She controlled herself, though not as well as Rosie had that day at Conkwell when she had stood on the nail with her bare feet and swore in a similar manner.

The Home was surrounded by emergency vehicles: fire engines, ambulances and police cars. Their wheels had gouged huge ruts in the immaculate lawns, their lights were spinning around like flails. Residents stood around draped in blankets. Some of them were sobbing. One large bewhiskered person of indeterminate sex was comparing it all rather loudly to the Last Trump, and more than a few were asking *Why?* Others still were comparing it to the Bath Blitz and were definitely going to be magnificent in their distress and show the youngsters a thing or two. Dust was everywhere, and the house itself had the collapsed face of a stroke victim.

A face appeared at Eleanor's window before she had even applied the hand brake.

"Where's that Chant woman?" stormed the Manager.

Eleanor and Grahl looked at each other.

"Where is she?" the face at the window roared, all purple and panting. Eleanor pressed a button: the glass whispered down. She could smell gin on the Manager's breath.

"She booked a taxi," the latter continued, as if this was the most despicable act in the world. "Said she was off to meet a friend. Well you're the only friend the old crow's got!" Spittle gathered at the corner of the mouth; both cheeks were flame-red and you could almost see every individual pore. He'd never become a lady no matter how many hormone injections he had.

"Listen, I don't … I mean … what's *happened*? And why blame Rosie?"

A hand shot in the car and grabbed the young woman by the blouse.

"Don't you have any manners?" asked Grahl, reasonably enough, reaching over to the hand and bending the Manager's little finger back so fast and hard it brought a gasp of pain and a quick withdrawal.

"I guess not. But let me tell you this: Miss Brittle has resigned from your crummy place from this moment on, and has no intention of working her notice. And if my great-grandmother Rose Chant has come to any harm while under your so-called 'care' I will sue you personally for every red cent you've got."

Well, Eleanor's little chest with her firm young breasts puffed up with pride and she burned with love; she felt as if she were soaring on love's flames toward a nearby heaven.

"Oh and by the way …" he added, leaning across to shove his head toward the Manager's, "you'll have heart attack soon and almost die. And in about 10 years time you'll wish you *had* died, and no-one will care." He gave a curt nod to his delighted driver and she spun the wheel, doing a u-turn where they had always been positively disallowed, flattening some rose bushes but not at all concerned.

"You sounded just like Rosie then," she marvelled, hurtling down the drive and entering the traffic stream with scarcely a glance to either side.

"Must be in the genes," he smiled, tapping out 192 for Directory Enquiries on the mobile phone. "You know her. Does she really have the powers the Journals suggest?"

Eleanor thought. She remembered all the little incidents and rumours, all the atmospheres and gossip. "Well, a lot of people believe she does. Yes, *I* believe she does! Now I do!"

"Oh hi," he said to the operator, reaching into the glove compartment with his free hand for the local map. "I'm looking for the number of any local taxi firm …"

* * * * * * *

So Rosie sat in the back of an old taxi, pulled through her dreams by a sort of Kellaway, and it was as if she riffled the pages of old light's chronicles: incidents, moods, chances and regrets, paths and tracks, faces and features, ups and downs of a lost age flickered through her mind's eye, triggered off by each new turning in the Lanes. Even the alterations of decades served to remind her of things which had slithered away, like a grass-snake she had once studied amid the corn when the world was young, before Himself appeared. They drove through the Lanes and the vessels of her heart, and no taxi meter yet built could have put a price on *that* journey.

"Stop here," she said, and Dulcie did. The narrow, steep road into Conkwell fell away from the passenger side of the car like a ski slope.

"You want to go down there?"

"I must," said Rosie, winding down her window with some effort but no complaint. Across the valley and among the trees she could see lights flashing below a pall of what looked like smoke.

"Well I'll drive you down and back up. You can't manage that hill. I couldn't."

Rosie shook her head, made a negative gesture with her hands, and the car stalled. Frowning, Dulcie did heroic things with the ignition but everything was dead and little red lights on the dashboard made cryptic signals that she had never bothered to learn. When she looked back to say something to Rosie the old lady had already gone, was halfway down the hill, the wad of money left in her place and irresistible.

"Missus! Missus!" shouted Dulcie, feeling vaguely responsible; the other woman never twitched. Deaf old bat, she thought, starting to fiddle with the ignition again. "Dead as a bloody do-do" she said aloud, but the bundle of notes stuffed firmly into her money pouch took away all rage.

Down at the well itself, nothing much had changed. The angled light had turned all the windows into silvered sheets again; the grass and shrubbery seemed greener and the colours generally more intense, like something out of her visions. A breeze rustled some exotic hedging where once there had been low and ornate iron railings, but it brought her voices, whispered *hellos* from the long dead. We would have seen the little green around the well as empty: to Rosie, it was a carnival. They were all there, everyone, as if the spring waters which leaked reluctantly to the surface had brought the old souls out from under the hill with them. Mum? Dad? *Mum?* The child within, Rosie in bud, was waking into the strange light of her last day. Years, decades fell away. She held her hand up to the sun and could have sworn from the rays which pushed between that her fingers were straightening. She went to the well. The water in it brimmed to the edges of the trough and seeped over like the tears in her eyes, like the memories in her unconscious and the ghosts in her visions. No-one could have read her thoughts then, or understood her feelings. *Water is a symbol of our consciousness, and what lies below it* said Grahl once. Rosie was among the aquifers, in the deepest levels and darkest caves below the hill and within her own soul, where all things began.

She heard a bell tolling from somewhere: golden snatches of sound carried on the tides of the air.

"Time to go," she said, taking a deep breath before leaning into the hill and heading back up the way she came.

* * * * * * *

"There!" cried Eleanor unnecessarily, for the taxi blocked the road, they couldn't have missed it. "I was right," she told her lover. "It was my Auntie Dulcie who picked her up!"

Her Auntie Dulcie was looking under the bonnet of the car with no clear idea of what she might be looking for. Really, she was wanting a man to come along and have mercy and fix it, and maybe ask her out to dinner also – who knows?

"Elly!" she cried in delight, and then looked wonderingly with one eyebrow clearly raised at the powerful car and its impressive passenger. Greetings were made; brief explanations. Responsibilities were passed over like Olympic flames while traffic built up behind.

"Try it again," said Grahl, and it started first time. Aunt and niece registered their surprise and shared looks.

"Did she say where she was going?" asked Eleanor who had been infected by Grahl's sudden sense of urgency and who suddenly felt as if they were perched on a far steeper slope than that which fell away in Conkwell.

"No … well to be honest she looked half-dead, breathing heavily after that climb. I wanted to call an ambulance when I saw her but she waved me off, said she was fine."

"She's going to Jug's Grave," said Grahl, squinting at the road as though Rosie had left snail-tracks which glistened in the afternoon sun.

"Where is it exactly? And how do you know?"

"I know," said Grahl in answer to both. "I just know."

* * * * * * *

In the maps of old light, crafted by the cartography of experience, the road from Conkwell to No Man's Land, and thence beyond it the short distance to Jug's Grave, is measured by the mundane genealogies of the working man, rather than the old Imperial system of yards, feet and inches.

Rosie walked through it all: the shadows of the aeons and all their people; the aeons of people and all their shadows: all alive at either side of her consciousness like the avenues of stone which she had glimpsed in one of her lives. The stone circle was broken, its monoliths up-ended or half-buried, scattered either side of the tarmac, but a side of her still saw it as it was and always will be within the dragon's eye.

Amid the trees to her left a scattering of New Age travellers' vans and caravans. Clothes lines stretched from branch to branch. Hens scratched at the mud. A young girl saved from school held an old dog on a string and made a pattern on the ground with a box of salt, snot streaming into her mouth.

"Are you lost?" asked this young child who belonged to no one place on this earth. She yanked the dog back to her side and made it cough.

Rosie paused. Despite the pains in her chest which – for once – had nothing to do with love, she smiled.

"Not any more," she said softly, reaching into her pockets for the rest of the money she had stolen.

"You look like a witch," the little girl said to Rosie, who stood where Heggerty had once stood. Again the smile, more forced this time. "Are you a good witch?"

Rosie-in-Hecate held out her hands full of notes and silver and flashes of gold, and offered it all to the child, who fastened the dog to a sapling and took the riches, wonderingly. Rosie walked on, though not so steadily. Behind her (or was it at the back of her mind?) she heard a young voice crying "Mum! Mum!"

Over the stile with some difficulty and into the vast, bare field of dark earth. She turned to her right so that the forest expanse of Inwood ranged behind, while before her the old cottage lay somewhere in the distance, beyond her failing eyes, across that vast expanse of mud and melancholy. Unreachable in this life now. She swayed and one heel squirled a pattern in the mud. *Not yet!* she implored to all the Powers within the Lanes and beneath the Hill, demanding their support for a little while longer. The breeze dropped. The day became still. She fingered the plastic poppy and felt something like her own self again. *But soon* she conceded, for Rosie at her death had a job to finish and The Man to meet.

*   *   *   *   *   *   *

"She's in there," said Grahl as he and Eleanor, holding hands, stood at the stile and looked first across the open fields and then back toward the woods which lined them. "This is Inwoods. Jug's Grave is in there."

Eleanor drew back a little. The holding of the hand which had been so wondrous to Rosie and The Man was no great deal to her generation. And her lover's voice was suddenly deeper, older and more absorbed, like an old man with reminiscence and marvels of his own. The moment was unnaturally still, as though they stood in a glass bell-jar. Crow after crow was gliding toward them and landing with a flutter to strut around on the bare earth. For a panicked moment she felt that there must have been hundreds, thousands, but her rational mind told her it was surely only dozens, though in constant and silent motion. Mourners at a funeral. Last respects.

There was a broken down fence with a sign saying **Private. No Admittance**. Two black bags full of dumped rubbish were snagged on the wire. The interior of the wood was dark, dank. She felt as if her brow was being swept by cobwebs, and her teeth started to chatter in response to a cold that was not in any way connected to climate.

"I'll stay here," she said as he climbed over the wire ignoring the sign. Grahl said nothing, didn't even look.

He's not himself she seemed to hear.

✳ ✳ ✳ ✳ ✳ ✳ ✳

You would need the huge eyes, elevated perch and night-vision of Hecate's owls to see what happened next: the sort of eyes that can see movement where human eyes cannot, over great and dark distances. Like Hecate's owls, whose pupils can respond to light from the most distant stars as well as the dragon-light of old Time, we have to see things at different levels, in differing ways. The mundane can be filled with magic; the trivial can glisten with muted splendour as the present swallows the past, and futures are reborn.

Human eyes would show us an old lady in a blue coat with her hood up, sitting primly on a damp mound amid shadowy woods, as matter-of-fact as if she waited for a bus. Her hands rested on her lap, holding the milk-bottle top like an OAP's token, ready to offer payments of another kind. An old hare limped past, unconcerned by her presence. Leaves fell in spasms, and spiralled down. And those same human eyes would see a young man stumbling through the undergrowth, muddying his shoes and tearing his expensive coat. Yet Hecate's owls high on their branch, whose pupils dilate to other light and receive inner frequencies, would see beyond or within: they would see the stillness; the blue-robed priestess of the hill and its Mysteries, awaiting the slow and ceremonial approach of her priest.

Stillness, silence. The sun diffused between the trees like mist.

"You've come back," said Rosie in a quiet voice, too shy to meet his gaze. "I knew you would." She reached out a hand but dropped the little disk on the floor.

"Allow me," said Edward Grahl again, bending down like he did that very first time they met, picking up the disk oh-so-gently and examining it with a wry smile.

"It's the Luck," she explained. "The Luck of the Hill. It should never have left. You should never have left."

He nodded. He was finding it hard to swallow.

"No ... no I shouldn't," he agreed at last, the words coming out with difficulty, a quaver in his voice.

Whether he was possessed or reborn, or shouldering family responsibilities, only the owl could have said, for those roads signposted as **What Was, What Should Be**, and **What Is** had all converged to this central point within the dusk, amid the woods, on top of the hill.

"There are the bones of a man and woman in here," she said, indicating the mound on which she sat. "They're thousands of years old. They loved each other hard ..."

Grahl, kneeling at her feet, raised her face to his and it was like the moon rising. Her silvered eyes, brimming with tears, shone.

"I loved you hard, Rosie Chant. I did, believe me I did. But sometimes ..." His voice trailed away like the carriage which had carried him off into the west on her birthday, when she knew she was pregnant.

She sighed and nodded. On Winsley Hill – on all hills everywhere – the roads you must take are rarely those of the pretty way, or straight way. She was priestess of the hill: she knew that. Her old bent hands cupped his face at either side.

"You haven't changed a bit," she said, and no-one had ever loved more, or more wonderingly, than she did then. Grahl mirrored her action and gently touched her face.

"I love you Rosie Chant," he insisted, making all things right at the last. She pushed back her hood. She was a girl again. She shone.

The air around the mound shimmered; everything seemed to be in soft, pastel colours. They were surrounded by presences: the entities of light and lineage that linked their destinies through time.

"Put it back," said Rosie, holding up the Luck she had made, seeing it glint with an inner light of its own. Grahl took it carefully, found a crack in the mound and pushed it in, making sure not to bend it.

"Thank you," she whispered, as he sealed the crack with earth. "Thank you very much ..."

He sat next to her and put his arm around her bony shoulder. She snuggled her head onto his chest, her breath coming heavily, though not from any passion.

"I'm sorry Rosie ..." His tears splashed on her grey hair. Tears that were a symbol of his own consciousness, and the conscience that lay below it.

"You came back," she sighed, and that was all that mattered, all that ever mattered. She was freed from Tartarus at last and was striding through meadows of light. Somewhere in the near distance a flock of crows was rising to the sky.

"Rosie? Edward?" cried a faint voice. And again: "Rosie! *Edward!*" It might have been Eleanor calling. It might have been the Spirit of the Hill. The sound flitted between the trees and seemed to whirl around them.

"Goodbye," said Grahl as he felt her old bones shuddering into release. Slowly, gently, he pulled the hood onto her head and laid her on the mound, curved like a child on her mother-earth's belly.

Hello said her voice inside his head as her radiance flowed into that which encircled them.

Rosie-in the-earth, happy at last.

POSTSCRIPT

A replica of the 'Sun Disk' which was taken from Jug's Grave can be seen today in Devizes Museum. Jug's Grave itself has become much damaged over the decades and sits in private grounds. No-one should try to visit without asking permission from the owner first.

Lightning Source UK Ltd.
Milton Keynes UK
UKOW02f0659170916

283208UK00001B/60/P

9 781908 011008